Crab Walking & Other Stories

By Judy Gorham

Cover Art by Gregory Gorham

Table of Contents

Dedication

While putting this book together, I thought a lot about my parents Roy and Lillian Grush. While watching my engineer father and how he went about his life, I learned a lot about being organized, how important it is to plan ahead and to note every detail. Mostly, I learned the wonder of solving a problem. My school teacher mother introduced me to the joy of reading when I was three. She read to me tirelessly and took me on endless trips to the library. The best thing she did for me, though, was this: she read everything I ever wrote with patience and enthusiasm. This book is for them. My mom winked at my dad on the train; that wink sparked a lifetime together.

Acknowledgement

I would first like to acknowledge all the people who have passed through my life and left little acorns that have grown into towering oaks or at least small bushes that I have planted in my garden of stories. My love to Mom and Dad, of course, to whom I have dedicated this book. I was inspired by Christie Krug who was my first writing coach upon moving to the Northwest. Also in my writing group were Jeff Tanner, Julia Wero, and Joleen Wasche who all contributed to my sense of what needed to stay on the page. Others who have encouraged my writing are Valerie Wagner, Gypsy Martin and Melody Matthews. And finally, I want to thank my sister Cyndie Grush for her constant encouragement; Jan Bono for assuring me that self publication is perfectly legit; Marty "Qwa" Brown for his patience in helping me record my audiobooks; and my kids Chris, Lizzie, Tyler, Hilary and sweet Jen who is no longer with us except in our hearts. And then there is that first reader, Gregory Gorham, whose patience with rereads was immense.

Thank you all!

Crab Walking

"It seems I'm not married anymore," Helen whispers to the mirror. The brush in her left-hand hovers above her head. After twisting her wrist, the paleness of her ring finger catches her gaze. Naked and fragile-looking with its untanned band of skin, it stuns her. Since it is only three weeks since she took it off, she is still shocked when she realizes how strange and solitary her finger feels without her wedding band. She has caught herself occasionally gasping when she has glimpsed where it should be, thinking it has fallen and is lost.

Her eyes move up the mirror to her face, where her glance stops. She recognizes this as the same face, the face to which he had said, "I do." Still the same face he had punched four months ago. The bruise has faded, but she still feels it high on her left cheek.

Helen's heart, too, feels damaged. If she could see it in the mirror, it would be crushed, and she is sure of this. Her life is plainly shattered. She resumes brushing. Her thoughts in these quiet moments are always unnerving, unexpected, and unwelcome. This sudden blinding recognition of her status halts her in her steps repeatedly.

She does a mental rundown—the words she no longer uses. There are many: "Husband," "our," "together," "we," and even "always" and "forever." These words have a joyful ring, evoking feelings she no longer shares with the married world. Her new vocabulary consists of words like "single, "failure," "alone," and "just me." She hates these words, but still, they identify her status. She longs for the right to the old, deceptively easy ones that fell off the tongue without a thought. Until they did not, of course. They

3

were simple and magical—words that did not make anyone look up with surprise, like the dreaded "Table for one?"

There are quiet times when she misses even the arguments, the sound of voices and emotion, the exhausting attempts to stay strong, and the robust electricity that once surrounded them both. Her life feels so silent and aimless now without someone to please, plan with, and share even the bad things, someone who may have laughed at her expense, but still, the laughter! She misses the laughter. Once all those things had made her days go by. They kept her life from stopping altogether.

She is positively joyful over the loss of in-laws, those unhappy, bitter people her husband brought into her life. She finds that, rather than acting out of spite now or because someone insisted, she can indulge in things she chooses just for the sake of pleasing herself.

She no longer spends her days worrying about their mysteriously disappearing money, items suddenly lost, what she may have done wrong, or even the news or the weather, which were both apt to set her husband off. She loves the absence of dread coloring each breath, each thought, each day from dawn to the dead of night.

Her greatest gain has been time—all the blessed hours she has gained and now spends without worry. Worries she had had about what she would wake up to each morning before leaving for work, about how big a mess she may have found when she came home at the end of the day. And that biggest time consumer that is no longer part of her life—those hours spent tossing in bed, awake and fearful, ever on edge; that constant vigil, the watchful hours, the fretful thoughts of his spending what little money they had on drugs or drink at the clubs where he performed, when he might come home, who he was with. No more! All those hours and minutes are now hers to spend on what matters to her, even if it's sleeping.

In the short four months since Helen asked Tom to leave, she has at last come to realize just a few moments each day of not being afraid, of not being cautious. She is aware of more time each day that is her's alone, time spent grounded in herself! She just is not used to being alone, planning alone, and living alone. That's all. "In time," she tells herself, "in time."

She mourns the dreams that never would have come true. She grieves for the girl who stood in her filmy white dress, filled with hope and dreams. That lovely girl promised to love, honor and cherish. Helen so regrets the loss of that girl's innocence and promise, missing now for years and years.

As she continues brushing her hair and trying different ways to tame it, her cell phone suddenly plays the little tune she assigned as Tom's ring eight long years ago. She looks at the display and sees his name, his picture. She remembers how she loved him when she added this entry to the new phone as soon as she had held it in her hand, a newlywed filled with excitement and joy. She has had four phones since that little flip phone, but the same ring has been used on each phone, at first raising hopes with its jingle but over time, provoking nothing but worry.

Helen hesitates. She picks up the phone, only shaking minimally, presses the little green light on the screen, and holds it to her ear. Into the phone, she says, "What do you want, Tom?" She is proud that her voice is almost steady.

"Mrs. Riley?" a stranger's voice replies. She wants to answer, "No!" However, of course, that is still her name. She acknowledges that she is indeed Mrs. Riley.

"Mrs. Riley, this is Sargent Simmons at the Copeland Police Department. There has been an accident on Hwy 92. I am sorry to tell you that your husband is in the hospital, hit by a drunk driver. I am calling to tell you which hospital he's in. It would be a good idea for you to head on over there. Are you okay with taking down this information?"

Helen stiffens. She sees red. *Why now? Why now?* She hears her own voice within the confines of her brain. *After I finally broke free of him, he has found a way to get back into my life! Why did he ask the police to call me, of all people?*

5

"Mrs. Riley? Are you there? Are you okay?"

"How bad is it, officer?"

"I am afraid he's in a coma. His truck was totaled, and he isn't doing so well. The doctors want to see you immediately to help make some vital decisions," the Sargent says.

"A coma!" Helen shrieks, completely unnerved by this turn of events. She wishes she could scream, "I don't want him! I don't want this responsibility! Call someone else!" But of course, she can't scream any such thing. Though separated, they are still legally married. Unless he has changed something, she has power of attorney for his healthcare. She will have to go and talk to the doctors. "Where is he?" she asks at last.

Propelled by nerves, Helen drives, crying, actually weeping. Her knuckles are white on the steering wheel all the way to the hospital in Copeland. Too soon, it looms before her, lit up like a Christmas tree, an ugly cement block. The flaming neon that spells EMERGENCY litters the wet parking lot with sharp slashes and trails of red reflection. She pulls in and parks badly. Her goal has been to park. In no way had it been to park well.

At the emergency desk, a nurse treats her indifferently, directing her to Intensive Care. Arriving there, she is confronted by a hushed crew who whisper and defer to her, the woman they assume is riddled with fear. She is ushered into a room to wait for a doctor. She is not taken to see Tom. In reality, she's relieved. Would the sight of him, even in a coma, set her on edge? Make her shiver? Make her stomach turn? Frighten her? She does not need to know.

A man enters the room wearing a sparkling white coat. He goes straight to the X-ray display, jams a film in the rim, switches on the light, and turns away. He does not introduce himself. He indicates the X-ray of someone's head, an anonymous skull.

"As you can see, Mrs. Riley, your husband's head is basically crushed." Helen could no more see that than she could read

6

Chinese, but she stared at him dumbfounded and shook her head to indicate she understood perfectly.

"Mm, Hmm, go on," she manages to say.

"Now, we'd like to ask your permission to harvest his organs for transplant. I know that sounds a bit offensive when he is still alive, but that is the only way we can do it—with viable organs. There are so many people that can be helped with your husband's aid. It can add meaning to his life." He shuffles papers and finally seems to locate what he wants. "We have counselors who can talk you through it if you want to donate, hmm…" he glances down at the top page, "Tom's, yes, Tom's organs. Or if you prefer and have already decided, you can just sign these papers." He shoves a disordered stack of papers toward her. His face is expressionless. This is not an emotion-filled moment for him she can see—just another day at work.

She is shocked. *What if I still loved my husband? What would he do if I threw a fit, went into a long wail?* She stares at him in disbelief. Even though Tom is not a treasure, he is a human being. This choice (and this doctor's presentation) befuddles her.

"I can't decide this without consulting his family," Helen says. She knows Tom's parents will despise her no matter how she chooses if she makes all the decisions about Tom without talking to them. She hates the idea of calling them! They will surely find some way of blaming her for Tom driving alone, at night, in winter, and even for the accident itself. Was he at a gig? Was he drinking or on drugs? That will not matter to them. Habits seldom change. Ryan and Betty have always blamed her for everything that went wrong in her marriage. All of their ridiculous accusations and messy emotions will definitely push her and her feelings to the rear of the room. Though well deserved, all their grief and sorrow will make her feel unnecessary. This whole situation will become their own personal drama, having little or no, connection to her or even to Tom.

A voice continues ranting in her head. *Thanks a million, Tom,* the voice screams.

Standing in the hall of the ICU, Helen watches the world continue around her. Nurses rush by with tapping rubber-soled shoes and technicians push carts attached to pumps and test equipment. A man and woman hurry through the corridor in scrubs, masks, and little blue paper booties. Their heads are bent in consultation, close and serious. Bells ring, lights flash, machines whoosh and rumble, yet everything feels ordered and dim. Helen touches the button to swing the double doors wide. When they whisk open, she makes her way out of Intensive Care. She cannot wait to escape.

Rummaging in her purse, she discovers she has forgotten her cell phone at home. She remembers throwing it down after the sergeant from the Sheriff's Department called her about Tom's condition. She goes in search of help. A nurse directs her to a bank of phones. She searches her memory for her mother-in-law's phone number.

"Hello?" She hears Betty say in her shaky voice.

"Betty, this is Helen." She listens as Betty sucks in her breath. They have never gotten along, but it is even more unbearable between them since she and Tom have separated. "Betty? Is Ryan there? Would you ask him to get on the extension or put me on speakerphone?" Too late, she realizes that Betty likely will not have any idea how to put the phone on speaker. Still, it would be easier for Helen to say this only once. Maybe Ryan knows how to do it?

No such luck. In an abrupt and cold voice, Betty says, "I'll find Ryan and get him to pick up the extension." Helen hears the phone drop and then muffled voices. At last, Ryan picks up the phone, and she hears the TV's monotonous drone behind his voice.

"What is it, Helen?" He says. "Why do you need us both on the phone, for heaven's sake?" There is a rattle and a sigh, and Betty is on the line as well. She says, "Yes, what in the world is the matter with you now?"

There is no earthly reason for Betty's reaction. Helen has barely spoken to them in six months. She has never asked for anything from the pair of them. She sighs just as loudly as Betty. She clutches the handset tighter.

"Well, Betty." Helen pauses. "I've asked you both to be on the phone because of an accident. Tom's rolled his truck and is in the hospital. They called me because he carries his cell phone, and it evidently still shows my number as his emergency contact."

"What hospital?" Betty's voice has become so tense and shrill that it nearly cracks the line. Helen fears she may start a prolonged howl. "How long have you been there without calling us, you wretch? Where is my son?"

"Now, Betty," Ryan's deep, slow voice censures her. "Just give Helen time to tell us what's going on, and then we'll go over there. What is going on, Helen? For heaven's sake, just tell us how Tom is!"

Silent tears spring from Helen's eyes. She is frustrated with the situation, her in-laws and their predictable ways, with herself for not getting divorced years ago, with Tom for clinging to life.

Her in-laws' distress makes her suddenly conscious of the terrible seriousness of the situation. She has been making this all about herself and her feelings when there are more far-reaching consequences of this accident. Hard not to do, but still, his parents, his life, it is so much!

"He's in a coma," she says as calmly as possible. "He looks gaunt, hurt, bloody. He is not even aware of his surroundings. Oh God! They've asked me to donate his organs!" Upon saying those words, her voice breaks.

It has begun to feel like a nightmare, a bad dream, some awful imaginary occurrence. But she knows it is a far cry from fantasy. Helen peaked into Tom's room before exiting the ICU. He had been white as a sheet and bruised. His eyes were swollen shut, his nose large and purple. He was covered to the chin in sheets, tubes

9

connecting him to monitors and machines. She did not even know if he were all in one piece. There was blood on his skin, in his hair. A pump breathed near the bed. He looked so pathetic and small.

"Where are you now, Helen?" Ryan is asking her. "Which hospital did they take him to?"

The ice begins at Helen's feet. Her lips go white and cold. Her knees buckle, and her eyes roll back in her head. She has fainted. The phone drops from her hand and swings from the coiled steel cord.

A nurse happens by and picks up the receiver. With her hand on the side of Helen's throat, she calls for help and then gives directions to Tom's parents. Helen is lifted to a gurney and whisked into a room where she is put to bed. Her vital signs are good, but she does not respond immediately. Her heart just isn't in it.

~~~~

Helen is aware again only when she hears the squeak of a hospital cart going by outside the door of the room. The hospital staff has put her to bed though she cannot remember why. She is lying beneath a couple of sheets, shivering, in underwear and a hospital gown. She remembers talking to Ryan and Betty. Then nothing.

She reaches for her glasses and sees the call button. She presses it. In a few minutes, a nurse comes to her room. By this time, Helen is up and putting on her clothes and shoes. The nurse is not sure this is a smart move, but Helen knows that Betty and Ryan will arrive soon, and she does not want to be slouching around in bed when they arrive.

"What happened anyway?" She asks the nurse.

"I'm not sure, Mrs. Riley. One of the nurses found you on the floor by the phones. We were not sure what might have happened, so we took precautions and brought you here. Your vital signs are fine, though. I don't suppose you need to stay." The nurse turns her back as if to leave Helen alone with her decision. Helen is not so sure.

"Can you wait a minute and talk to me?" She asks. "I feel a little shaky, and besides, I'd like your input on something."

In the next 10 minutes, Helen tells much of her story to the nurse, Esther. Esther, it turns out, is a fountain of information. She has plenty of experience with patients' families making the kind of decision that Helen, Betty, and Ryan will be making. She is not emotional, and that helps to settle Helen.

Still, she cannot decide on a course of action.

~~~~~

Once Helen is dressed, Esther gives her a glass of orange juice before letting her go. Helen drinks the juice, thanks Esther, and goes out the door. She walks carefully down the hall to Intensive Care.

~~~~~

Outside Tom's room, Helen catches sight of both his parents and a doctor she has not seen before. As she is approaching, Betty is grilling the doctor on Tom's condition and his chances of recovering his mental capabilities. Even though Helen hears the doctor say that Tom is not ever going to regain his ability to speak, walk, think, sing, play the guitar, drive, or do anything else a normal human would do, Betty catches sight of Helen and says loudly to Ryan,

"So, it sounds like we can count on Tom's 100% recovery very shortly. Oh, Helen, did you hear that?" She looks at Helen with a stunned and vacant expression. Helen turns to Ryan and raises her eyebrows.

11

"Really?" she says. "Is that what the doctor said?" The anonymous doctor is suddenly gone, having ducked into the room where Tom's quiet body rests.

Helen follows the doctor into the room. Betty tries to push her back out the door, but Helen just glares at her. Tom is quite a vision. He is attached by tubes to bags, rolling stands, and machines at the bedside. There seem to be plastic cords and tubes everywhere as if a giant spider has been busy locking Tom in. The small beeps and boops seem deafening to Helen.

"Doctor?" Helen says, "Doctor, do you have any questions for me? I'm Tom's wife."

The doctor turns to face her. He looks astonished. "Wife?" He says. "I was under the impression that Tom's folks were his only family."

"Well, no. I actually have Power of Attorney for Tom's healthcare," Helen tells him. "Tom has no insurance and a history of drug and alcohol abuse which I believe you should be made aware of."

Betty gasps. "What have you done with Tom's insurance?" She demands. "And how dare you insinuate that he has a drug problem? How dare you, you conniving woman!"

Helen whirls around and confronts Betty.

"Betty, for the last eight years, Tom had no insurance that I did not supply. I paid plenty to keep his policy paid up through my job. Every month the payment was so high I had to scrape together to pay our rent. Every month! When we separated, I could not pay it anymore and also afford to live on my own. It was Tom's business if he did not want to buy his insurance!

"As for the drug and alcohol abuse, well, he's been doing drugs for years. He picked up habits while performing late at night with other musicians in clubs that don't close until the early morning. As for drinking, Tom drank when I met him and was still drinking when we split up."

Helen has never said anything to anyone about Tom hitting her. Though she knows it was not her fault, she still feels humiliated and embarrassed that it ever happened. She is injured to the core because, in her heart, she knows his fist testified to how much he did not love her, how little he valued her. She feels there is no point in mentioning it now.

In a moment of clarity, she sees how her statements have hurt Betty, whose son is near death just a foot away from them both. She sees the pain in Betty's face, her eyes so worn out with worrying. She cannot take her words back, but maybe she can soften the blow. But, no, Betty stiffens her shoulders, and Helen knows the moment when they may have connected is gone, shoved aside by Betty's stubborn and unforgiving attitude.

"Ladies, please, don't talk this way in front of Tom," Ryan says quietly. He touches them both on the shoulder. His face looks tired and sorrowful, a look well earned from his life with Betty but more so now with Tom's condition. The doctor, meanwhile, slips out the door and closes it, essentially turning his back on this family and their personal problems.

"I think we should discuss this situation," Helen says. "But I agree with Ryan. We should go out in the hall to talk."

Betty looks at Helen like she is a senseless brick. "Discuss this situation?" she squawks. "Talk about it?" Her voice rose. "What exactly did you want to talk about, Helen?"

Ryan, his hands still on their shoulders, firmly guides them out the door and into the hall. The man in the white coat who first spoke to Helen shows up just then. He looks expectantly at Helen.

"Have you decided on your husband's organs?" He says, eyebrows raised, hands full of forms. Betty pulls back and gasps. Helen considers where he picked up his tips on timing.

13

This doctor, who has the strange and unpleasant job of acquiring human organs for transplant, leads the three of them to a conference room. He can see that they have no basis for this kind of decision and will take some persuading. He fetches a social worker and some coffee. The door shuts with a thud. At last, he introduces himself. It's easy to see he's been in this chair before.

"I'm Dr. Pembroke," he begins. "Your husband and son, Tom Riley, was injured beyond recovery in this accident on Highway 92. The cause of the accident and its particulars are not important to this discussion, so I will just tell you a little about what my job is.

"When there is an accident in the local area and one or more of the healthy victims is injured as badly as Tom, we ask if the family would like to donate his organs. If no family is available, we consult the victim's driver's license and go with what was requested by the victim on the back. Now, Tom indicated that he wanted to donate his organs in an accident as severe as this one. However, his wife, Helen Riley, has his Power of Attorney for Medical Care, so she has been consulted.

"Mrs. Riley did not give us an answer, preferring, she said, to wait and discuss this decision with you, his parents." He nods at Betty and Ryan. They both look like train wrecks. They stare at him. In tandem, they turn and stare at the wall.

"What I'd like you to consider is this: There are registries all over the country with patients waiting, sometimes for a very long time, for organ transplants that can save their lives. People like your son, Mr. and Mrs. Riley, can save or help a dozen people with organ donation. Tom's brain has been monitored, and the results show next to no brain activity. Thus, his chances of recovery are next to none.

"What I'm asking is if you would be willing to allow us to harvest Tom's organs and ship them off to locations where someone can benefit from a transplant. I hope you will consider this. I know it's not an easy time nor a simple choice."

Dr. Pembroke looks each of them in the eye before continuing. "This is Caroline Drake, a social worker. She can assist you with any questions regarding this program and help you to make the right decision today. She is experienced in this line of work and knows the forms inside and out as well as the answers to legal questions you may have."

After the blunder of their first encounter, Helen is impressed with Dr. Pembroke. He has spoken intelligently and shown that he knows how to communicate with people who are suffering. However, she can see clearly that Betty and Ryan are not leaning toward an agreement.

As Dr. Pembroke gathers his papers and turns toward the door, Betty pulls her purse from the back of her chair and rises. Ryan stops her with a touch to the arm. She sits back down. Ryan looks at Caroline Drake. He is thinking. Helen holds her tongue.

~~~~

Several hours later, Helen stands alone at the counter in the hospital cafeteria, pushing along a tray with coffee and a sweet roll on it. She reaches for a napkin and fork, counts out the money she is asked for, and takes a seat by the window. It is dark, and the glass is cold. It is probably getting close to daylight. The cafeteria is fairly deserted, with only a few lone diners, most of them hospital employees on break.

Helen looks out at the parking lot. She glances up at the stars still showing through the skylight overhead. She sighs and puts sugar in her coffee and stirs.

They have broken her resolve. She cannot seem to stand up to Betty's tortured grief. She thinks of the lives that may be lost, eyes that will not see, skin left burned and painful, a heart or lung that could save someone's happiness or life. Meanwhile, Tom lays, barely alive, in a bed hooked up to machines for however much time he has left. She thinks about what she would want someone to do for

15

her, to release her from the useless life that Tom will now face, to let her go when she's done, and make use of her leftover parts.

Betty cannot be persuaded to let Tom die. She insists he will get well, that his life will resume, that his treasured voice will once again sing out. In the conference room, she had cried and wrung her hands. She had insisted on the strength of his spirit. How could she let them take organs from her living son? How could she? And how could Helen ask such a thing?

She had turned on Helen, making her feel it was all her idea to begin with. It's as if Helen arranged this accident so that someone somewhere could benefit from Tom's demise.

Ryan sat, meanwhile, silent and gloomy. His neck bent, his head hanging low toward his chest, he had refused to participate in the discussion. Helen believes he is already in mourning for the son who, though he did not perform in life as Ryan wished, was nonetheless still Ryan's son, still his only offspring.

Helen and the social worker Caroline, have both tried in vain to change the minds of Tom's parents. Helen knows she can act without their agreement but fears she will go to hell if she does. They are Tom's parents, after all.

At last, papers unsigned, Betty and Ryan had returned to Tom's room, and Helen went to find something to eat, having not tasted anything but coffee since lunch the previous day. The sweet roll is tasteless. She takes a few last crumbs up with her damp finger and eats them in one swallow. She covers her eyes and sighs.

Then she gets up and goes to Tom's room.

~~~~~

There is activity here, at least. The Rileys have agreed to disconnect the pumps and tubes, and so on. Helen has convinced them that if they believe so much that Tom will get better, they should allow him to breathe on his own. The social worker had not liked that idea, but she was outvoted. Betty is sure he will survive. Ryan is doubtful but still would prefer that his son be untethered from the machines.

The choices they have made for Tom have been made without the help of a lawyer or another person who might know the ins and outs of this situation. They are, all three, going on gut instinct. They have not considered what will happen next. For now, they are just concerned with getting Tom off the machines. And that is just what is happening.

While Betty and Ryan hold Tom's hands and Helen hangs back, trying unsuccessfully to think of sweet memories, the nurses are unhooking the pumps from Tom's body. A drip is discarded, needles taken from his arms. The mask that covers his nose and mouth is removed and disconnected. More is done, things Helen does not understand. There are so many people involved and so much activity that Helen loses track. It is a quiet affair with glaring white lights. Helen's eyes are burning.

In the end, only the monitor is still connected. Like a young rebel, it continues to beep, the hilly pulse line continues to go up and down, and Tom's chest continues to rise and fall.

Tom does not die.

While all in attendance hold their breath, Tom does not hold his. He keeps breathing in and out, his heart continues to beat, and his brain remains lost in eternity.

~~~~

At 6 AM, after Tom was disconnected and continued to breathe, Helen left the hospital to run home for a shower and to change her clothes. Later she returns, perhaps expecting Tom to be gone. She finds that he has been moved to a ward. Betty and Ryan have posted themselves as sentries at his bedside. They have been there for hours and wear the same clothes they wore when Helen

17

left. She wonders if they have even been home, if they have had a meal, even a nap. They do not say. She does not ask.

She, at least, feels somewhat refreshed by a shower and a change of clothes. In the light of day, she wonders if what they did was the right thing to do. She looks at Tom, her heart filled with resentment. She wants to punch him for surviving. She wants to scream at him for making her ask his parents to give up his organs. She looks again and sees a bludgeoned and woeful stranger in the bed.

She turns and leaves the room without saying a word. In the hall, a woman comes up to her with a clipboard clutched to her bosom. Her I.D. badge reads "Samantha Cooley, Hospital Administration".

"Are you Helen Riley?" she asks. Helen nods, and the woman continues. "I'm Samantha Cooley." She puts out her hand and waits to shake Helen's. "I'm in charge of your husband's case. It appears he has no insurance, so I wanted to talk to you about payment."

Helen balks. What is she talking about? And why? Why now?

She stares at Samantha Cooley as if she had just popped out of an egg. "What do you mean?" she asks.

"Well, Mrs. Riley, Mr. Riley's bill is getting pretty big. Without insurance, you are responsible for his bill. We cannot keep him here indefinitely without payment arrangements. So I need to know your plans. Are you going to arrange transportation to a nursing facility?"

"I don't know what to say to you," Helen says. "I have no plans. I cannot afford his bills. Have you talked to his parents?"

"I did," she says. "I talked to them about an hour ago, and they said it was up to you. Whatever arrangements you wanted to make were fine with them. That's what they said."

18

"Will you please excuse me?" Helen replies. She turns and reenters the ward. Tom shares this room with three other occupants, all asleep in their beds with curtains drawn. She walks through the room and pulls aside Tom's curtain. Betty and Ryan look up.

"What happens now?" She says to them. "Did you stop last night to consider what would happen when Tom had bills to pay?" They both look at her blankly.

"Well, he's your husband, dear," Ryan finally replies. He turns away and looks angelically at Tom in bed. His sweet and mild ways are such a cover. Betty grimaces or smirks; Helen cannot tell which. Then she takes Ryan's hand, pressing her cheek to his sleeve. They stand together, looking to Helen about as stupid as any two people can look.

~~~~

Helen goes to the desk and asks for Samantha Cooley. She is told to go to a room on the third floor, and a call is made to ensure Ms. Cooley is in her office.

As she walks in the door of Ms. Cooley's office, Helen says, "I don't know what to say to you. I am lost. Can we just go over this state of affairs?"

"Sure," says the ever-cool Ms. Cooley. "Have a seat, and let's see what we can come up with."

Together they go over Tom's bill; his bill so far, that is. It is astronomical. Helen is shocked at the amount charged for each and every second of his care, each pill, each inch of bed space, it seems. The ambulance ride alone is more than she makes in three days of working full time.

Helen explains that she and Tom have been separated for several months. She tells Ms. Cooley that Tom works in nightclubs and gets paid by the day, seldom more than it costs him to live for exactly that one day. She explains that when they separated, Tom

19

was supposed to get medical insurance or at least apply for Medicare or Medicaid, but he evidently did not do this. Basically, she can't pay.

Ms. Cooley listens intently. She nods and says things like, "I see." In the end, she simply tells Helen she can apply for government aid if she so desires, and Tom's bill is due now, though she can work out a payment schedule with Helen if that would help. Lastly, her husband should be moved from the hospital today. If they have a plan for his next place of residence, the hospital will help with transportation arrangements, but she will also have to come up with the money for that.

"If you would like to meet with a social worker, that can be arranged," Ms. Cooley says. "I believe there is someone on the floor at the moment who can talk to you. Would you like that?" At the moment, Helen doesn't like anything, but she agrees.

~~~~

What it boils down to is this: Helen will have to take Tom home. There is no alternative. She can't afford a nursing facility, she realizes, and she can't leave him where he is. She is stuck with the hospital's astronomical bill and also with the man in the bed.

She goes back to her in-laws. "Can you help me?" she asks them, at her wit's end. "Can you spare a little money to help with the rental of a hospital bed and a wheelchair, or maybe help me pay to have a caregiver come to the house?"

Betty and Ryan confer. "We can't help you," they say. "We're on a fixed income. We have nothing to spare."

"What about time?" Helen asks. "Can you afford some time to help with Tom? I'm going to have to go back to work full time in just a few days in order to pay for everything since Tom has no assets."

"No," they tell her. "We just aren't in any shape to take on the care of a man as big as Tom." Helen knows this is true, but she had to ask. Betty has trouble doing the laundry and lifting pots to the stove. Ryan lifts nothing all day save the newspaper and, now and then, a golf club. Any help they would offer would be so minuscule it would not be worth the time she would have to spend telling them what to do.

Despite their urgent pleas for their son's life, Ryan and Betty flinch at the thought of Tom's predicament. They are really no more nor less help than they were when Helen and Tom were married and living together. If Helen had agreed to have Tom's organs removed and donated, he would, of course, have died in the process. Still, she did not sign the papers when he was on life support, and now that he is breathing on his own and does not require technical assistance to stay alive, there are no papers even to consider. Helen is married again, married to a nearly invisible partner, one who requires lots of care but offers nothing in return. A partner she was in the midst of divorcing.

~~~~~

Three months pass. Tom does not regain consciousness. He makes no demands. He does not argue or complain. Tom is like a pet cat, but an expensive one. A pet requiring someone to drop by and change its diapers once a day while Helen works. A pet that requires turning, fresh sheets daily, sponge bathes, a special diet, IVs and medicines, and a warm heating pad. Tom remains in bed, sleeping or not sleeping. Every day is the same.

But not for Helen. Her job presents her with a lot of responsibility and stress. She loves her job, but it is almost all consuming. She also has a small but cherished personal life. That, however, seems to be over. She makes many excuses and repeatedly tries to forgive herself for shortchanging those near her. She rushes everywhere, trying to squeeze more out of a minute than is possible. Helen is overly busy, and she quickly burns out.

21

Despite their wishes to avoid helping Helen, she calls on Betty or Ryan for help from time to time. "Ryan," she says when he answers, "would you and Betty be able to come by for just an afternoon visit?" He barely replies. "No," he says and hangs up. A week or so later, she'll call and ask Betty, "Can you come to see Tom for a few hours this weekend so I can get some shopping done?"

Betty's replies never alter. She and Ryan are always much too busy. They cannot help her even for an hour.

But twice weekly, at their convenience and unannounced, the older Rileys come by to visit. They refuse to be left alone with Tom, but they do seem to want to see him. On one such occasion, when Betty comes by herself, she looks mournfully at Helen and complains, "Helen! Tom's tan is fading, and his beard has grown all scraggly. His blanket has a stain, and it's rumpled. Can't you do something?"

"For God's sake, Betty!" Helen exclaims. "Why don't you take him to the beach in your spare time? Hire a couple of strong men to pick him up and place him nicely on a beach towel. At the very least, if it's so important to you that Tom looks his best, you could give your son a shave. Or, you know, wash his blanket, maybe?"

Betty turns white. "How dare you talk to me like that! It is your job to take care of Tom! He is your husband! Take me home right now."

"Why do you even come here, Betty?" Helen asks. She stares at Betty, obviously puzzled. "What is it you want? I know it has nothing to do with visiting Tom. I suspect you just want to check up on me— to make sure I haven't let Tom go to pieces or, even more likely, to be sure I haven't let him die."

"You've always been a terrible wife, Helen. That is why Tom is in this shape. This is your just reward for not living with Tom in the first place. After all, you made vows! You promised to stay with him until death." Betty is nearly hollering, she is so irate.

Helen turns to Betty and glares. "You sit right there!" she demands. She turns to the phone and calls Ryan. "Come and get your wife," she says. "Come pick her up before I throw her out in the street!"

Ryan dutifully comes and picks up Betty. They turn and walk to the car without a word to Helen. Something feels different. Helen has begun to feel stronger than her mother-in-law.

~~~~

Several more months pass. The bills mount. Helen does her best, but it's just too much for her to do it all alone. She has worn herself out with caregiving. She has spent all her savings. She feels she is working for nothing at all. She is so far behind! Every day she feels like she is just crab walking, continually going sideways and never getting anywhere.

She has lost weight, and her clothes are too big, but she cannot afford to replace them. In an effort to retain her sanity, she begins to talk to Tom. At first, she rants. She complains. She goes on and on about how unfair her life is. Then, finally, she grows empty of feelings, and she calms.

Helen contemplates ways to save money. At first, she stubbornly refuses to see why it is up to her, but she gradually decides to be sensible and figure something out before she gets too far into debt. She looks out the window and sees her little car, the one she is so proud of and worked so very hard to buy. She takes out a paper and a pencil and starts to jot down the expense of keeping a car: the payment, insurance, renewing her license and her registration, maintenance and gas, car washes, and the new tires she will need soon. She pays an additional $30 a month for rent on the carport.

She sits at the computer and looks at the webpage for the local bus service. A monthly pass seems reasonable. Tom can also qualify for the dial-a-ride program to take him anywhere he might need to go. She had never considered what would happen if he did need to go somewhere, and she would have to get him out the door and into her car. Dial-A-Ride would be great.

She talks to herself for an hour while she folds clothes. When she is finally finished, she goes online and uses the one and only credit card Tom had in his wallet to buy herself a bus pass. She applies for the Dial-A-Ride program under Tom's name. Then comes the hard part: she lists her car for sale on Craigslist. When she turns from the computer, tears are dripping off her face onto her T-shirt. She sees that Tom's blankets have slipped, so she goes to his bed and straightens them, tucking them in to keep them snug and in place.

~~~~~

On her first day riding the bus, Helen walks two blocks to the bus stop, carrying all the things that used to be thrown in the back seat of her car—her lunch, purse, book, notebook and pen, calendar, mittens, and an umbrella. Today they are all together in a tote bag. She feels unrested and just wants to nap, but it is time to sip her coffee from the portable cup she'd picked up at the Goodwill. It is time to gear up for work and get her head out of the apartment and into the world at large.

Though she does not realize it, she is one of the lucky ones this morning. She has a seat. Many other riders have to stand and hold onto a strap, and though their ride might be short, they sway uncomfortably during their trip.

Helen notices how people maintain privacy while sitting so close together in such a small space. She watches as people board the bus and take a seat. Many immediately open a newspaper or a book. One woman takes out a notepad and starts writing, and a young man sketches in a tiny journal. She feels out of place, but she knows she will soon figure out this mode of transportation, which will be familiar and comfortable. She realizes she needs to find a way to make use of this time. Because it is her first bus ride, she is afraid she will miss her stop, so she does not read or make lists. She keeps her eyes on the way as they go.

The ride is much longer and more distracting than when she drove, with the stops and starts, the opening doors letting in a breeze, people getting settled, and so on. There is a kind of rhythm to it, and she feels she might dose off if she does not pay attention. Things do not look familiar, and the route is not the one she would normally take in the car. She glances at the map across the aisle above the heads of those seated there. She counts stops. Then, she sees her building coming up and is thankful the bus stops just half a block from it.

Going home at the end of the day, she drops into the only empty bus seat with such relief. It feels good not to face traffic, to let someone else dance with the cars, trucks, lights, pedestrians, and streets.

On this very first day, she sees Mandy. She does not know Mandy yet, but soon they will be friends, bus friends, that is. Mandy has slipped her shoes off and is rubbing the tops of her feet along the back of her calves, one at a time, her head back, and her face tired. Turning, she sees Helen watching her and smiles the warmest smile Helen has seen in months. Her face lights up and her eyes twinkle—literally twinkle. Helen blushes to have been caught watching. She smiles back and then looks away.

As the days and weeks go by, Helen continues to take the bus to work and back. She finds a certain peace in the travel along the same route, seeing the same people and sights. She remembers the days of driving to work, listening to her radio and crying over the words in the songs, daydreaming of what might have been, what might eventually happen, fighting traffic, and looking for parking. But while riding the bus, she is always armed with a book, her calendar, and her notebook. So there are days she reads or writes, making a grocery list or writing note cards. And there are days she just zones out, sitting in blessed peace.

Somedays, she is lucky enough to get a window seat. She looks into the homes along the way, studies other neighborhoods, watches children playing and lives going on, passing by her window

25

like a movie. She wonders what life is like for the people she sees. She cannot imagine anyone with a problem like hers. She cannot conceive that there could ever be a support group for people in her predicament. She is sure she must be the only one.

~~~~

After not hearing from Betty for a few weeks, one day, Betty calls. "Helen," she says, "Ryan has been very sick the past two weeks. Kind of weak and tired. I didn't call you because I knew you wouldn't bother to tell Tom, so what would be the point? Last night he went to the hospital. He had a heart attack and died in the night. He is gone. I am just devastated. I cannot believe he is dead! I do not know how I will live without Ryan! He was my rock!"

Helen's first reaction is disbelief. She hears nothing, and then, unexpectedly, Betty calls with this horror story. She knows they are not close, that no matter what they never will be. But to keep all this information from Helen and Tom, no matter his condition, is remarkably strange. She is right. Helen would have seen no reason to tell Tom, but Ryan was his father.

She pauses, not knowing what to say to Betty. Her tone had been so matter-of-fact in the telling. What could she offer? It is not something one does every day, speaking to one's mother-in-law on the event of her husband's death. At last, she settles on kindness.

"Betty, I am so sorry. You and Ryan have been together for so many years. It must be like losing a limb! I wish you had called me! What can I do to help?"

Betty laughs. She actually laughs! Then she tells Helen, "I'm going to go visit a friend in California right after the funeral. I need some time away from here. I am exhausted from caring for Ryan and worrying over Tom. What help would you ever be to me? Goodbye, Helen."

After she hangs up abruptly, Helen sits and thinks this over. What a turn of events. She feels freedom— free to handle things her

26

way without worrying that Betty might suddenly show up. Helen is tired of trying to please Betty, a woman she can barely stand and certainly does not want to deal with if there were a choice. That night, after considering everything in their lives, Helen decides to make some changes to their routine.

Though Helen's workload continues as before, she makes an effort to spend more time talking to Tom. She tells him about his father and how sorry she is that he has lost his dad. She talks about Betty going to California for awhile, though she doesn't know how long that will be. She reads aloud to him books he would never have read but ones she wants to read. She leaves the radio on for him during the day while she is gone. She lets Tom's hair and beard grow, something she knows he always wanted to do, though his mother would certainly object. When she leaves in the morning, she sets his guitar on his bed and lays his hand on its neck. She slips her wedding ring back on just to feel connected in some way to the man she cares for. She tells him they will manage.

And they do. They manage.

~~~~

Twice in the first month of riding the bus, one stop after she has boarded on her way home, the lovely Mandy has boarded the bus and taken the seat beside Helen. Though Helen has seen her several times before, she does not look directly at her. What she can see is that the woman wears sensible shoes and dark slacks, neat and pressed. Her handbag does not have a shoulder strap nor a brand name stamped all over it or a tag hanging conspicuously from the handle. She notices how the woman smells of hand lotion and lemons and how regular her breathing is. She has pretty hands but no ring. What she knows from watching her board the bus and from across the aisle is that the woman is just of average height and build, her skin a gorgeous chestnut color, and that she has big brown eyes and a wonderful smile.

A few days after Ryan's funeral, which Helen reads about in the paper, Tom is finally approved for disability, and checks will

27

soon start coming in the mail to help pay for his care. When the disability approval letter arrives, tears of relief pop from her eyes. She will be able to arrange two visits per day by a healthcare worker instead of one. She can buy big puffy blankets for Tom and pay back bills she was worried she would never be able to afford. She wonders in her heart if Ryan is behind this change of events somehow. She is grateful if he has handled it, wherever he is.

The third time Mandy sits by Helen is just a week after Ryan's death. She walks down the aisle of the bus smiling with just one dimple and brilliant white teeth. Helen realizes that the woman is smiling at her! Her eyes sparkle. Helen instinctively smiles back but then catches herself and coughs, turning her gaze back to the window just as the woman takes the aisle seat next to her. She sighs loud and long.

As they ride side by side, their shoulders touch from time to time as the bus turns corners or changes lanes.

"Excuse me," the woman says. Her voice is warm and soft, low and comforting. Helen can imagine her singing to inspire tears; her voice is so rich. Helen turns a bit to face her seat companion.

"I'm sorry," the woman says. "I know people don't often acknowledge one another on the bus, but I've sat beside you a few times and feel it would be nice to know your name to greet you." She pauses. Extending her right hand, she says, "I'm Mandy."

Helen is surprised at her pleasure. She was growing so tired of the sterility of her commute, and she realized how much she had been craving conversation with another woman. Her job involves spending all day in the company of men, machines, computers, and calculators. She goes home each night to another man with his machine. A woman seemed just the right interruption to her static life. She takes Mandy's outstretched hand.

"I'm Helen. It's nice to meet you, Mandy. My best friend in grade school was named Amanda, so your name won't be hard for me to remember." Helen is so happy about this distraction. It's been a tough week.

"Hmmm," Mandy hums. "I'm not an Amanda, actually. My name is Mandolin. My parents were musicians and folk singers. My father died before I was born, and Mom named me after his instrument. It's kind of poetic, don't you think?"

Helen is intrigued enough by the story to turn half in her seat, the better to see Mandy's face. "It is! What a great way to remember her husband! It must have been a comfort to your mother, having his musical legacy live on in her child."

Mandy's smile deepens. "Well, yes, I guess it was a comfort to her, though at times I was not such a comfort!" She covers her mouth and giggles.

Helen feels a chill and pulls her jacket closer. Dare she dream of having a friend? Should she stop talking to this woman right now? She didn't want to give up this chance to have someone, just one person she could talk to from time to time about things besides work details or laundry, medicine, medical machines, and turning her husband over to avoid bedsores. Just a few minutes a day. Why shouldn't she have that? Well, she should! She should, and she would.

"Why the big sigh today, Mandy? Was this an especially hard day for you?" It felt so good to ask someone a question and to know that they would be willing and able to answer you.

"Well, you see, I work for a big manufacturing company that makes cleaning and personal supplies. I answer the phone 8 hours a day. It's one of those 800 numbers on the side of a product jar or a package. The messages say, 'If you have any questions, you can call….' Well, that's me. I am that person you would get if you called."

"Really! I never thought those calls actually went to a person, and if they did, who they went to. So, it's you!"

"You're not alone, Helen. Few people think they will get a real person when they call. But I'm here to tell you, they do! And you know, usually, I get folks with real questions like 'Will this

29

shampoo hurt my dry scalp' or 'What makes your detergent smell like lemons—is it lemons or chemicals', things like that. But today, I got this call from a young-sounding man. His question stumped me."

"What?" Helen asks. "What did he ask you?"

"Here's what he said," Mandy answers. "'How do baby birds know they should fly?' That is what he asked me. How do baby birds know they should fly? Just like that. On our question line. Well, I do not know! I can tell you that. I felt so bad. I didn't know what to say — and that's not my usual problem!"

"So what did you say?" Helen asks her.

"If you give me your name and number, I'll look into that and get back to you.' It's our standard script to answer a question that stumps us."

"And?"

"And he did. His name is Wayne, and his number has a Chicago area code. It's hard to say where he is. He may have a Chicago number and live elsewhere."

"Oh, this is my stop." Helen stands. She bends and gathers her things. Before she gets off the bus, she looks down at Mandy and smiles. "See you tomorrow?"

"Of course," Mandy says.

Helen departs the bus and begins her two-block walk up the hill to the apartment where Tom waits. Where quiet waits. Her heart is lighter, but the walk is filled with dread now, and she is back in her boring cocoon in no time.

~~~~

Six weeks pass. Surprisingly Betty calls from California.

30

"I have met the most marvelous man, Helen! We are going to marry! He has a house on a cliff here in California, and we can see the ocean from the windows. I will lack for nothing. He buys me anything!"

"I also wanted to let you know that I'll be living here, so I have hired someone to come and close down my house. To sell it. To ship me all my things. I don't see any point in keeping ties with the past!"

Helen feels a blaze of resentment and anger. "You amaze me, Betty," she says. "Every time you open your mouth, you amaze me more. You know Tom is part of your past. Are you planning never to see him again as well? Is he now classified as 'the past' and no longer necessary for your future well-being? Or maybe I misunderstood—do you want me to ship Tom to you, too?"

"You are not going to ruin MY happiness, Helen. I have finally been rewarded for the good life I have led. I am not going to argue with you about my choices." Betty hangs up, clearly believing this will end the conversation and any tie she may possibly have with Helen or even her son.

Helen turns and bitches to Tom. She complains that she is shackled with her supposed ex-husband, who was thrust upon her for care by destiny, and her mother-in-law, and now here is her mother-in-law finding a new life and going off getting married without a care in the world for her son! Helen is glad Betty will not be back, but she is not happy with what her own life has become. She does not want Betty to be happy, especially not at her own expense.

Strangely, the ranting helps. She has gone on and on about how unfair her life is. Now a strange stillness settles in. She feels calmer, and the freedom and joy she had felt when Betty announced her intentions to go to California return with a vengeance. She feels more capable and in charge without Betty hanging over her shoulder.

31

Without interference, home life goes by but seems to pass too quietly. Helen does her best, but the isolation with no distractions is hard. She has a routine, but even that offers nothing. The ranting comes and goes. The loss of control in her life sets her back time and again.

Eventually, she stops talking to the walls, to herself, to no one or anyone. Tom is her only company from when she comes home until she walks out the door in the morning. The day she gets four bills in the mail that she cannot pay, she turns to Tom, lying in the hospital bed she can't afford and taking up her whole living room. She begins to holler at him, blaming him.

"Tom, you lazy big ass. You lay there all day while I am off working. People come in and wash you, change your diapers, and feed you. No one feeds me. No one washes me! And you are no company. You are just in the way! I am at my wits end on how to pay all these bills. Why don't you do something? Why? This is so unfair!" When she starts crying, she stops hollering and goes to sit in her only chair remaining. When Tom moved from their apartment, she dreamed of sitting right in this chair with a book in the evening. It was supposed to be comforting, a warm and welcoming corner for her at the end of the day.

"You have ruined my life, Tom." She is more controlled now, but her resentment is so huge she cannot contain it. She speaks quietly and evenly. "This cozy chair was my first purchase when we separated. It was to be my comfort. Now it is the only place I can sit in my apartment because of you, Tom. Because of you!" She blows her nose and tosses her tissue at Tom's bed. Of course, it falls on the floor.

She looks at him. She is suddenly struck with pity as she considers him in all his bedded glory. He did not ask for this any more than she did. "Why should I feel sorry for YOU?" She snaps at his prone figure. He does not move, of course. He is not really there at all.

The next day when she meets Mandolin on the bus, she looks terrible and knows it. They have continued to have small

32

conversations, their length defined by the traffic and time allowed between stops. Helen has felt the need to reveal more about herself, to tell Mandy parts of her life just to have a normal relationship with her. She is guarded, telling only small snippets of her life. But Mandy is so easy to talk to that she opens up more and more.

Mandy sticks to the bus rules pretty well. She does not pry, and she tries to keep it light. Helen loves to see her when she comes down the aisle of the bus each afternoon and has taken to saving a seat for her if she can.

They do not exchange phone numbers. They do not make plans to meet up after work or to go to the movies or out for drinks together. They just pass the ride talking and relaxing on the way home.

At first, it was awkward for Helen to talk to someone like Mandy, who was so bright and unafraid. She acknowledges that she lives her own life with her emotions running rampant under her skin. If one were to brush up against her, she might split open and spill her guts. But she is learning a kind of sweet peace from Mandy. It is a special way of letting things go that are just going to happen anyway. It has been such a valuable lesson.

Over the weeks, while they have become friends, Wayne has continued to call from Chicago. He has more and more questions for Mandy. He has asked her how flowers suck water up with their stems, what happens to puppies no one wants, and how art starts in someone's brain. Mandy has been stumped each time. She and Helen commiserate about the questions and who Wayne might be. They worry he may be ill or alone. His questions are so thoughtful and innocent. Together they think of answers to his questions that might be funny, but they do not think Wayne is funny or that he is making the calls for kicks.

One evening Helen returns home to find the caregiver has left her a bouquet of flowers in the kitchen. She is so pleased that she cries. There are few moments of goodness in Helen's life. While she arranges the flowers in an old pottery vase left by her mother, Helen tells her silent husband about the phone calls Mandy gets

33

from Wayne. She wants to talk about it with someone, and there is no one to talk to but Tom. She is so puzzled by the person making the calls and taken with the questions themselves. Tom does not protest. She can talk until bedtime if she wants. And so that is what she does.

~~~~

On the bus one morning, Helen feels a surge of warmth for Mandy and turns to her unexpectedly. It is so out of character for her to confide in anyone. She lives in a kind of bubble of shame over her living conditions though there is no reason to. It just feels like it needs to be kept private. But here is her new friend, Mandy, and so much is brewing in Helen's head. She cannot hold back.

"Mandy, I know I have told you I am married and a few things about my husband. You know he is a musician, and we have no children. But there is a lot I haven't told you."

Mandy holds up one hand. She smiles and says, "Helen, you don't need to tell me about your life. It's okay to keep silent about what you do when we aren't together, you know."

"I know," Helen says. "But I want to tell you this. In fact, I think it will help me, and I think I need to talk about it. Do you mind?"

Mandy does not seem to mind. She smiles.

"Tom," Helen starts, "Let me tell you about Tom—my husband." Helen twists the ring on her finger absentmindedly. "We were in the midst of getting a divorce when he was in a car accident and ended up in a coma. He lives with me… in a coma. He has been there for many months. Our life is sort of like the two of us riding around in a tiny closed car that no one else can enter… just me and Tom. When the ride ends, I will be alone, but I am afraid to say that that may not be so bad after what I have been living with."

Mandy interrupts Helen. Aghast, she says, "Helen! What? I cannot believe this is a true story! I am so sorry! I don't know what to say!"

"You don't have to say anything, Mandy. I did not want our relationship to be all talk about Tom, so I kept our conversations centered on the moment, on our interests—yours and mine. I like it this way. But you know, Tom is a huge part of what I do when I'm home, so I guess I need you to know about him if you are going to know me!"

"So he actually lives with you," Mandy asks. "in a bed?"

"Yes, there was no choice. There still isn't. There was just never enough money for him to stay in any kind of facility, so I just kept him home and had caregivers drop by a few times each day to check on him. It's all I can do. Well, that and bathe him and wash his sheets and feed him." Helen sighs and tries to laugh as she looks out the window.

"But what I really wanted to tell you is that our conversations have helped me stay calm and get on with my life as best I can without a nervous breakdown! You have helped me stay alive, and I want to thank you. You give me other things to think about and distract me from my isolation. You are such a blessing in my life, Mandy!"

Mandy pats Helen's hand and smiles her gorgeous smile.

That was on a Monday. By Thursday, Helen has thought of a way to save some money, but she is unsure if she can do it. When she sees Mandy, she knows she wants to discuss it.

"Hi, Mandy. How was your day? Any calls from Wayne today?"

"No, it was a quiet day. I only had a few calls. I really prefer it when it's busy because when we don't get many calls our office manager makes us file! Ugh! My back gets so sore, and my feet ache. But it's part of my job. How about you?"

"My day was good. I had an idea, though, and I'd like to run it by you if you don't mind giving a girl some advice."

"Good grief, Helen. I can barely run my own life, but I'd be happy to listen, and maybe I can help."

And so Helen begins to tell Mandy about her money shortages and what she's done up to this point to save what she can for when she might need it, as if the present were not that time!

"I'm not looking for pity from you. Let me set that straight right off the bat, okay?" Mandy smiles and nods her head.

"Here is what I was thinking about today," Helen says. "Tom has a tiny apartment a couple of miles from mine—you know, where we live now. It is just sitting there empty. I thought I might want to close it up and stop paying his rent. What do you think?"

"Helen" Mandy sits up straighter, and her eyes open wider. "Do you mean to tell me that you're still paying rent on an apartment that Tom lived in before his accident? Before he started living in your living room? For, like, over a YEAR?"

"Yes, that's about it, almost a year. I kept paying the lease out of loyalty or in case his mother asked to go there, so I wouldn't feel I had betrayed him or to prove that I felt he might one day get well. There are so many reasons, all pretty stupid. But altogether, the weight of the reasons became pretty heavy! At first, I did not even think about it. Then after his mom moved to California, I started to consider it a little. Then the other day, when some new medical bills started coming in, I just thought, 'What the hell am I paying that rent for?'"

"Okay, girl, you have to get rid of that apartment right now! Close it up and put whatever he has out at the curb, in storage, or your basement. Whatever! Just stop wasting that money! This is ridiculous. Eating ramen and paying rent on an empty apartment!"

Helen felt a weight lift off her shoulders. She knew Mandy was right. She had known this all along. But to do it, she needed someone to tell her it was okay. Since Tom would never be able to tell her this, and Betty would have had a fit at the thought, Mandy was the only one.

"Mandy, I told you, you were a gift, and you are! Thank you for this affirmation. I just wanted someone to say it was a good plan."

"It is the only plan, Helen. Just do it, for heaven's sake."

And so, after tossing the idea around, Helen decides to close down Tom's apartment and maybe store some of his things. Her outlook improves once the decision's been made. She will be able to apply his rent money to the amount she owes the hospital. She's known for a long time that Tom will never return to his apartment. What has been the point of keeping it? Making changes was just scary. She is thankful that Mandy agreed with her. It set her mind at ease.

The following Tuesday, when Helen has taken the day off work for a late afternoon appointment with a social worker, she gets up early and, taking some boxes along, calls an Uber to drive her to Tom's apartment. She's relieved when she finally arrives. Happy she wore a warm jacket, Helen enters the unheated apartment and glances around. She feels the sadness that still rests on every surface. The sorrow that was Tom's life when they split up seems to have settled in every corner, and though she knew then that separation was absolutely necessary, she feels sorry now for how alone he was here.

Going through his things is harder than she expected it to be. Once she has poked in the cabinets and seen his paltry collection of dishes and the closet that is nearly empty, she goes to the porch and brings in the boxes. When she opens his dresser drawers, she sees clothes she had forgotten—shirts that would now fall off his meager frame, socks tossed in randomly (a habit of his, she remembered), a funny hat he wore when he went out in the snow, a special T-shirt he bought at a concert they attended together.

She looks in places she would never have when they were together, married, a couple. She finds his memories, some shared, some not. It's an eye-opener for Helen. How sentimental he was when he collected the things he had tucked away.

In a drawer, she discovers a copy of a menu from the first place they ever ate together, a crushed flower she once gave him for his birthday, and the words to a song he wrote for her in high school. Who else would remember these things? She feels privileged, in a way, for sharing his most intimate remembrances and guilty for poking into his things. She feels strangely like his wife, setting his life aside in perfectly packed boxes. For whom, she will never be sure.

Helen heads to the office when she is finished, and the discards are in boxes at the curb, ready to be picked up by the Goodwill. When she enters, the woman at the front desk looks up at her expectantly. Helen holds up the key and smiles as best she is able.

"I'm Helen Riley," she says. "My husband Tom had an apartment here—number 3B. He was in an accident about a year ago, and it looks like he will not recover. I came over today to clear his things out and turn in the key. Can we do the paperwork so I can close his lease?"

"Helen, I'm Mary. I can help you with that. I'm so sorry Tom isn't doing well." When she turns away, Helen wants to laugh at her words. She wants to holler at Mary's head, "He's been in a coma for a year, Mary. I would say he's not doing well is an understatement!" But she holds back. Mary doesn't know and does not ever need to know about Tom.

When she turns back, Mary holds out a form for Helen to complete and sign. It's official looking and kind of off-putting. Helen does her best to get it done quickly, but she ends up in tears anyway. She is so sad after seeing Tom's little apartment and imagining him living alone there. She just cannot help herself. Mary asks her for her address and explains to her that they will get her a check for the deposit once they have inspected the apartment.

Helen calls for a driver and goes outdoors to wait for the car to take her to her next appointment. Tucked in her pockets and her tote bag, she carries the few things from Tom's apartment that mattered. There was so little. So little left of his life.

~~~

Their routine becomes very regular, especially as time goes on, and Tom becomes very weak. She has no surprises. Tom does not seem to change in her eyes. He stays in the hospital bed supplied by Medicaid, sometimes sleeping and sometimes not, never speaking or even listening, as far as she can tell. They make no eye contact. She cleans his hands and face. She cuts his toenails, an act at once intimate and businesslike. They make their way.

At times Helen feels as if she has been alone for a very long time. She feels like she is the widow of a living man. She will be watching TV, and when something funny happens, she laughs and looks over at Tom, realizing too late that he cannot understand. Instead, he lays there with his mouth open and his eyes glazed. She feels bitterness and sadness. She once loved him. She once thought the sun rose when he opened those eyes in the morning. She does not hate him now, but she feels held back from life, stifled and imprisoned. It is so hard, and it is so lonely.

On a Friday, the aide calls her at work. "Tom has a fever," she says. Helen wonders what that could mean. She goes home early to check on him. She finds him pink-cheeked and breathing hard. She phones for an ambulance because she does not know what else to do.

Tom goes back to the hospital. This time they do not ask about his organs. He has a fever. Who knows what could be wrong and what he might pass along? His meager insurance from the state does not pay for much, but it does cover the ambulance and a bed in a ward. She leaves him there, where she knows he is cared for. He will get antibiotics in a drip and some tests. And care. Care that she does not have the energy to give.

When asked, she signs a DNR and shows her ID and the papers Tom once signed to give her Power Of Attorney. She has no qualms about it but does not hope for his demise either.

When she returns, the apartment feels so quiet. Every few minutes, she wonders what to do next. The clock ticks so loudly that it's overpowering. Her purpose is all mixed up with Tom's, she realizes. After a glass of wine, she begins to see that this pause in life that she had been unable to name is just her marriage! The story of Helen and Tom includes this interlude of silence, this time of sharing but not sharing. They are in this boat together for better or worse. She is finally settled with that. She recalls the words to a song she learned as a child. "Row, row, row your boat gently down the stream. Merrily, merrily, merrily, merrily. Life is but a dream." She thinks this song is about her reality, her life of floating in a dream. It feels, unfortunately, like a nightmare.

Helen is shocked that she feels so exhausted. After the wine, she goes directly to bed. She takes time off using Family Leave and sleeps hours upon hours while Tom is gone. Her mind is clear. She does not dream.

Helen goes in to see Tom for a few hours every day, but then she goes home and sleeps some more. As she doses off, she thinks of Mandy and misses her. She misses her few hours of freedom each workday. Then she falls asleep and does not think at all.

The wisdom she has gained in her life as a caregiver gives her a new sense of worth. The tests she has put herself to have given her pride in her abilities and strength in her purpose. When Tom comes home, she will be ready.

Though Tom's state worsens, he is released from the hospital. The doctor recommends hospice. He says Tom may survive quite a while but likely won't. The infection has damaged his lungs and heart. Helen agrees and makes some calls with the help of a social worker the doctor recommends.

The hospice workers begin their parade through the lives of Helen and Tom. They dole out his medicine and take his vital signs.

40

They give him sponge baths (what a relief!) and change his bed linens. They put him in a wheelchair, something Helen could not do, and take him for walks. One of them comes by each and every day supplying Tom with at least two visits per day, company, and safety. A chaplain comes and spends time talking to Tom as he lays in bed breathing. They have a key. Helen never worries; she just goes to work knowing they will be there if Tom is in need sometime during the day.

One day when she sees Mandy on the bus, she finds her sad and quiet. "What is it, Mandy?" she asks. "What could make you so sad that you don't even talk to me?"

"Wayne called me while you were AWOL. He wanted to know why life was so hard. I felt like an idiot. He is so serious. And he seems more and more despondent. I cannot stop thinking about him. I do not want to let him down. Why is life so hard, Helen?"

"Why is life so hard?" Helen says. She pauses and tilts her head, thinking. "Well, that is the question of the hour, Mandy. Life is hard because it's work, I guess. Life is work from morning till night. It is not a party. Sometimes it seems life will keep getting harder and harder, but then something wonderful occurs. Like me meeting you! That was wonderful. That is all we can hope for from life—that something fantastic will occur occasionally. It can and often does keep us going. Maybe something like a big red rose in the middle of a plain bush—just a flash of brightness. Tell Wayne. Tell him to keep looking! I'm sorry if that breaks his heart."

Mandy stares at Helen for a minute, then reaches over and takes her hand. "What happened while you were away, Helen? I didn't even ask you."

Helen looks down at Mandy's hand. She is afraid to talk for fear her voice will crack or a tear will escape. She works so hard at being strong, standing on her own, and never sharing her fears.

"While I was away from work, Tom got a bad infection and had to be hospitalized. He has come back to the apartment on hospice. And don't get me wrong, hospice will be such a big help,

41

but I just don't know if that is the answer. It was a hard choice, and I just don't know what I really want."

When she looks up, she sees that Mandy has not judged her. She continues to hold Helen's hand until Helen's stop appears. They do not say goodbye. Mandy squeezes her hand, and Helen gets up and leaves the bus.

A month after Tom starts hospice care, Helen calls Betty and gives her an update on Tom's condition. Betty seems indifferent. She thinks hospice is uncalled for when there is Helen to toe the line, but she does not seem to care all that much. She has her new life, her new husband, and her house with a view. She focuses on that and not much else.

Tom's condition changes slowly, going from not-so-good to pretty bad. Riding home on the bus, she tells Mandy things have worsened for Tom. She tries not to always talk about him, but he is constantly on her mind.

"Helen," Mandy says, "I want you to have my phone number. I want you to call me when you need to talk or when you need help. Please. It's okay for us to be friends even if we did meet on the bus!" She gives her an envelope, and Helen tucks it in her coat pocket.

"Thank you, Mandy. Thank you so much." Helen looks out the window and turns quiet. She watches other neighborhoods, houses, playgrounds, schools, and offices slip by. She thinks about their peaceful appearance, yet she knows something is always happening there. Life is not just a quiet view from the bus. Life is action. Life is busyness. Life is sad, and life is happy, and life has love, loneliness, joy, good news, and bad. There, out that window, Helen sees life as her bus rolls on by.

Walking home from the bus stop, Helen feels the envelope in her pocket. She had all but forgotten it. She takes it out and opens it. At the top is a stamp that says Mandolin Harmony Sherman. Her address is listed under her name, and then she has written her phone number for Helen. She writes: "Call me anytime, night or day. Call me! Don't hesitate. I mean it! Mandy"

Helen realizes she never knew Mandy's whole name, let alone her home address or phone number. She knows that Mandy means what she says. She is so honored to be Mandy's friend. She touches her name and smiles.

One night after work, after dinner and dishes, when Helen usually reads to Tom, she hears Tom's breathing change. He gurgles and rattles and seems in distress. Because hospice care does not allow doctors or ambulances, Helen calls the 24-hour hospice number.

"Tom sounds really strange," she says. "His breath is coming in gulps, and he has a rattling in his chest. Is there something I should do?"

Someone at the hospice office very kindly helps her through Tom's last hours. "Tom has some hard work to do now. You should stay close and tell him everything you have neglected to say. This is your last chance, Helen."

They tell her, "Try to make him comfortable. He may grow chilled. Can you see his pulse in his throat?" She tells them she can. "When that little dip stops bumping up and down, his heart will have stopped. Look at your clock, then. That will be the hour of his death. You will need to know this later when we speak. His breath may continue for a while or may stop first, but the heartbeat is his life's signal.

"Stay with him, now, Helen. You don't want him to be alone for the start of this journey."

Within a few hours, Tom's heart stops beating, and Helen steps out onto her balcony to send him on his way. She raises her hands in the air and says quietly, "Be free, Tom. Let go of this lifeless body and be free!" She cries for the miracle of life and death and how life slips into death with such distress and yet so much ease.

Helen calls her friend Mandy. "Can you come over? Tom is gone. I need something I think you can give me." Mandy does not hesitate. She is soon at the door.

By the time Mandy arrives Helen has given Tom a sponge bath with sweet smelling soap. Together they put fresh pajamas on his emaciated body. They cover him up in a quilt from his grandmother. Helen lights a candle, and then they sit together with him for a few hours before Helen finally calls for the cremation company to come and pick him up.

Helen is so thankful for this friend she can be comforted by, for her company and love. After Tom's body is taken away, Mandy fixes Helen a bite to eat, a cup of tea. She sits there with her as long as Helen needs her company. Then off she goes, leaving Helen with her thoughts. A hush settles in. Helen sits in her special chair and cries until morning.

The next day, which seems so soon, people from hospice come to pick up Tom's equipment, hospital bed, oxygen machine, medications, etc. They are noisy, hollering to one another from the hallway, the truck, and the living room, crashing the equipment as they fold it up and wheel it away. Helen makes calls to inform people she thinks will care that Tom has passed on, musicians from his past and high school friends. Few people have kept in touch with her since his accident.

At 5:00, she sits with the phone and a very special bottle of wine. This wine was one she and Tom bought long ago to celebrate something fantastic they imagined would happen one day. Something so special that it never occurred, and so they never opened it. Now she opens the bottle and pours a glass for herself. It turns out to be delicious.

She calls Betty. In Betty's time zone, it is only 3:00. She has just come in from the store and her card games. She is busy getting ready to make dinner.

"Betty," Helen says, "Well, there's not much to say. Tom has died. I guess that's about the best place to start. He had a fever, and after a few weeks, it was apparent he wouldn't make it. I am so sorry for your loss, as well as my own."

"I'm very busy right now, Helen," Betty says, being her usual caring self. "I can probably find time this evening to call you back but don't feel you have to bother me with details."

When Helen hangs up seconds later, she knows she will have nothing more to do with Betty in this lifetime. She has done her best for Tom. She has tried to be a good wife and follow through with the promises she made at their wedding. But Betty? Well, Betty was not part of the bargain. Neither she nor Tom ever mentioned Betty when they married. Betty has become part of Helen's past.

~~~~~

A week later, the phone rings after Tom has been cremated and the ashes returned to Helen. Helen is very tender. Her feelings are so close to her skin that she cries over a broken coffee cup. When she hears Betty's voice, she wants to disconnect right away. There is nothing they have to say to each other.

But Betty feels differently. She tells Helen that she and her new husband will be out in a few days to pick up Tom's things. "Just leave everything as it is," she says. "Jerry and I will take care of it all."

Helen pauses for a moment, and finally, words come from her like lava from a volcano.

"Betty," she says, "You can just stay where you are. You never bothered to come and see Tom when he was still alive, and now you want to show up to claim his things. Don't bother! Tom had very little, and what he did have, I have given to the Goodwill. I rejoice that I never have to see you again. When I finally get around to sorting out his few possessions, I will forward to you what I think you deserve, but really, Betty, I would not hold my breath. It's doubtful that there is anything that would fit that description."

When she hangs up, Helen feels a huge weight lift from her shoulders. She knows now that her marriage is finally and truly over, and her life without Tom can begin where it left off that day when she caught sight of her naked ring finger in the mirror. Strangely, she feels more married to Tom than ever before. She feels the loss of never talking to him again. She misses caring for him and doing what she thinks is best for him. She feels his absence in the immense silence.

She slips her wedding ring off her finger and goes to the dresser. In the top drawer, she opens a box and puts the ring inside, resting alongside an old menu, a crushed flower, and a song a young man once wrote for her.

Mr. Harvey's Surprising Adventure

Sheila's right breast is up against Mr. Harvey's left arm. He's sure of it. He tries not to look. He closes his eyes and concentrates on the warmth. It's a healing alternative.

There's a flurry of motion on his chest where the paper bib protects his clothes. Some rustling. And then he feels some pressure when she reaches across his chest for an instrument or something. He cracks his eyes and sees Dr. Payne's huge thumb approaching from the right. When fingers grab hold of his tooth, his head is nudged back into the headrest. The fingers start yanking, and his head shakes from side to side.

"Hold still, Mr. Harvey," Dr. Payne says without moving his lips. He tries to be still but feels himself bite down. "Don't close your mouth now," he is admonished. This is getting to be aggravating. He just wants to think about Sheila and her warm scrubs-covered breast leaning against his arm.

"We're going to have to deaden his mouth to get this work done," the dentist tells Sheila. "Go get me a blah blah blah." Mr. Harvey has no idea what the dentist has asked for. He hopes Sheila does. "You can sit up now and rest a minute, Mr. Harvey. We're going to deaden that area before we proceed. That might take a few minutes."

The bib is removed and set on a rolling tray. The chair vibrates and begins to glide slowly to a sitting position. Mr. Harvey's collar gradually pulls tight around his throat as his head rises. He has to readjust. He thinks he could choke. But he doesn't. Finally, the curved blasting light is no longer pointing at his face.

When he looks around, Sheila is not there. He's very disappointed. Even in rubber gloves, her hands are delicious.

Eventually, Sheila returns with a huge needle. Dr. Payne fools around with a long swab in his mouth. Mr. Harvey looks directly up the dentist's dark nostril. Then in goes the shot. Something tastes horrible. He doesn't feel much but suddenly doesn't want to have a stroke-like, saggy mouth. He regrets that Sheila will see him with a droopy lip. Ah, well, he supposes she's used to it.

Sheila and the dentist slip out the door and stand in the hall. He hears them whispering. At first, he worries they are talking about his case, that it's bad news, and they are working out how to tell him. But it's really only a tooth that needs work. How bad can it be?

Then he hears Sheila whisper, "I can't meet you tonight. I have to pick Frank up at 6:00. I can't be late. Don't start pressuring me, Jack!"

Jack! Mr. Harvey is alarmed. *I didn't know Dr. Payne's name was Jack! Oh my god, he's after Sheila! What a scoundrel. Pressuring his assistant for favors!*

"Keep your voice down, Sheila. You and I—the time we have--that's sacred. When will you have time for me, if not tonight?"

"I don't know, Jack. My life's a busy one. There are so many things that matter more than you and me."

"Matter MORE? How could anything matter more? You are the sun and the moon in my sky, Sheila."

"Oh, Jack, for god's sake. I am not."

"How's that lip coming, Mr. Harvey?" the dentist calls. Mr. Harvey doesn't think Jack really cares. There are more urgent things afoot. He tries to answer but is drooling, and the words come out slurred. He blows spit. The word "fine" assumes a life of its own and floats out to the hall.

The whispering continues. It sounds more urgent each minute. Finally, Mr. Harvey hears Sheila's nylon pants whisk whisk whisk down the hall. He is very disappointed. He hopes she won't be replaced with Angie. Angie is not his cup of tea. He thinks about rescheduling his appointment, but his lip is a mess. What else could he do with this day now that he has this sagging, lopsided mouth?

Payne returns. He seems troubled. Mr. Harvey hopes that his personal feelings won't interfere with his work as a dentist. Mr. Harvey doesn't want to lose another tooth. He closes his eyes again, and when he opens them, Sheila stands beside him with her hand on his arm.

"How are you doing, Mr. Harvey? Do you think you're numb enough for us to drill now?" Mr. Harvey is tempted to say no. He would like Sheila just to stand there and pat his arm for another hour. Or better yet, he would love for Sheila to lean her breast against him again and wait it out. He thinks about how they could console one another. But he sees she is distracted and would likely run off if he asked to wait a little longer. So he says he is ready, and Jack-the-dentist returns.

He sees Sheila pick up the suction device and lean toward his mouth. He hears that sucking noise coming closer. The dentist leans in from the right and pulls Mr. Harvey's mouth open. He pinches the lip. Mr. Harvey feels nothing in or around his mouth, but the skin near his eyes stretches obscenely. The dentist picks up the drill.

Mr. Harvey doesn't want to close his eyes again. He wants to watch Sheila. But he can't keep looking at her once the drill starts up. That horrible whining cuts into his brain. Not watching is his only defense.

Just when he thinks Sheila will lean into him again, he feels her body stiffen. She starts talking.

"You had better not have any notions about firing me," she tells Jack. "I'll sue you 'til the cows come home." Mr. Harvey is so pleased to hear her use this phrase. He hasn't heard it in years. He

49

thinks she is very brave. *Take that, Jack!* He squirms with delight. Then Jack answers,

"Don't threaten me, Sheila. I'm not going to fire you. Just do your damn job and stop giving me all this shit." Mr. Harvey is appalled. What kind of way is that to speak to your employee? This Jack is a really bad person. He hopes his mouth is not in danger.

"Fine...what time do you think you'll be home tonight?" If Mr. Harvey's mouth were not already open, his jaw would drop right now. *Whatever can Sheila mean by that?* His eyes move beneath his closed lids. Jack grunts.

"I forgot I have that meeting at the church after I leave here, so I'll be a little later than usual. Probably 7ish. Why don't you and Frank rent a movie? Would you hand me that other bit?" Sheila stirs the items on the bib again. He hears the sound of metal on metal as the bit is changed. The drill starts up again. He wishes he'd taken nitrous oxide. Or, at the very least, he had worn the headset with the pretty music. Nothing in the office seems real.

The work continues. Sheila speaks a few times. She mentions ham, macaroni, cheese, and a trip to the grocery store on the way home. She says she'll drop Frank off at the video store while she shops. The cavity is filled and polished. Mr. Harvey's head spins. He jumps when the dentist, Jack, finally pats him on the shoulder and says,

"You're all done now, Mr. Harvey. If you have any pain or discomfort this evening, give us a call. I don't anticipate any trouble, but you just never know."

"Where should I call you?" Mr. Harvey answers as the chair moves dramatically into an upright position. "At your church meeting or the home of Frank and your assistant?" He is feeling very disoriented. He wonders if it's the Novocain or the conversation he has overheard.

"My assistant is my wife, Mr. Harvey. Frank is our son. But you just call the service. They'll be able to find me at any hour. Now don't worry. You'll do okay." Jack walks out and leaves Mr. Harvey alone with Sheila, whose back is turned as she straightens the room and puts things right. She is so beautiful. He doesn't know how she can be married to Jack-the-dentist, of all people.

He cannot get the arm of the chartreuse chair to move out of the way. He struggles, and after catching his leg under it and then past it, he manages to rise. Shaking his head, Mr. Harvey makes his way down the hall to the red lights of the EXIT sign.

Drive

She packed her things in the new car. She had three days to drive. She wanted things to be different.

She brought a few clothes, a book, a notebook and pen, some cash, a bag of chips, and some cookies. She put her flashlight in the glove box, the tissue under the seat, and her sunglasses on the visor.

Driving, she had no plan. She opened the window and breathed country air within twenty minutes. She drove.

She had five CDs in her car stereo. She turned it on and started to sing. She harmonized. She sang the melody. Her hair flew out the window and curled in the wind. She sang and munched chips, and eventually, she had sung all the songs on all five of the CDs.

She started them playing again.

She saw a coffee drive-through up ahead and signaled. She pulled in and ordered a big latte from the barista. She dropped a dollar tip in the tip jar and drove on.

With coffee, cookies go better than chips. She opened the cookies and sipped the coffee, and ate some cookies.

Outside there were fields and some cows and sheep and some wildflowers. Big unkempt trees leaned this way and that. Old wooden fences lined the road. Mailboxes on posts leaned left or right. None of them stood up straight.

There were big billowy clouds in a sky so blue she could not remember ever having seen such a color. It was blindingly beautiful to this city girl.

She came upon an enormous banner welcoming her to a town she'd never heard of. Nearby was a sign for a B&B. She pulled over. It was a quaint little house with rose-colored shutters. She parked and went in.

After many hours alone, she found it hard to speak. She asked finally if there were a room.

"Oh, yes," said the landlady. "There are two rooms and no other guests. I don't get much business midweek. Would you like to see the rooms?"

She went upstairs alone to see the sweet rooms under the eaves. She chose the room that had pale blue wallpaper with tiny yellow flowers and a yellow chenille bedspread. By the time she had paid and fetched her things, a vase of yellow daffodils was on her dresser. She congratulated herself on the find.

What shall I do now? She wondered. There would have been no such question in the city. There was always too much to do! But here, here the question was just an opportunity to wonder and daydream. She took off her shoes, propped herself on the bed with her book, and promptly fell asleep. The window was open, and the room was fresh and cool. Sometime in her sleep, she pulled up the knitted throw from the bottom of the bed and covered up with it.

When she awoke, she could hear cowbells and mooing out beyond the vegetable garden. She got up and looked out the window. The cows were in a line, coming in to be fed or milked or to go to sleep. She really didn't know the habits of cows. But she did like the way they lined up and followed one another across a meadow and on towards the big red barn down the road.

Back in her shoes, the throw folded at the end of the bed, she went down the hall and used the shared bathroom, which of course, she wasn't sharing with anyone. Then she went down the little stairs and found the landlady knitting.

"Hello, dear," she said when she saw her tenant was up and about. "I was about to make myself a salad. Would you like to join

54

me?" And so she did. She helped. Together they cut up fresh garden lettuce, tomatoes, peppers, and celery. They chopped parsley and cleaned sprouts. Onions were fetched out of the back room, and carrots, too, which they added. It was a huge and fresh and gorgeous salad.

Rose, the landlady, had made a delicious salad dressing with sour cream, mayonnaise, and some kind of wonderful cheese. Then she opened the oven door, and there was a nice little roasted chicken. They sat and ate slowly and talked and drank big glasses of fresh spring water.

The question was finally posed, "Where are you going?" Well, that was a question, wasn't it? She told the truth.

"I don't know. I'm just going for a drive in my new car."

They did the dishes, packed away the leftover chicken, and called Rose's dogs. Off they went on a walk. The sun was setting. The sky had just enough clouds to make a glorious sunset. Rose told her all about the town when it began to be a town, who was who, and what was what.

That night she slept like a rock in the forest. The rooster woke her at 6:12 am. She sat up and smiled. She hadn't felt that smile for months. She could not remember what she last had smiled about.

She never went back to the city, of course. She stayed with Rose for a month, and then she got a little house to rent there in the nameless town. She got a job at the library and met everyone that had ever lived there, it seemed. She read every single book, and she smiled every day.

Morning Rush

"Oh, man! I'm going to be late again!" Colleen moaned as she set the dog's water dish outside. Nothing had gone right from the minute she got up. Emma had cried non-stop since dawn. Lunch meat had fallen on the floor when she went to make lunches. The dog barfed in her shoe. Six-year-old Larry couldn't find his ball. He had to have that ball! The kids were fighting over TV shows even before breakfast. Then Emma threw her cereal on the floor. Colleen just wished she was already at work and not in the Mom role at this moment.

It was the day to pay tuition at the preschool. She ran from room to room, looking for the checkbook. She just couldn't find it. She went to the desk and pulled a check off the next book in the drawer. She would just have to enter it in the register later.

"Kids!" she yelled, "Time to go. Let's get in the car." She heard thumping on the stairs. At least, she hoped she heard thumping on the stairs. Yes, she did. They came at top speed and in their jackets. She would have to remember to thank Larry for helping get Emma ready.

"Run and get in the car. Mommy's late again," she told them as they ran by her, giggling. As they opened the back door, the dog slipped back into the house. Colleen rushed over, pushed his little fat body back outside, and closed the door. She turned and gathered her things, opened the back door, turned the lock on the knob, and stepped out, slamming the door behind her.

In the garage, she was pleased to find both the kids in their seats. "What a relief!" she whispered as she neared the car door. Sweet Emma's eyes were red from crying earlier, but Larry had managed to cheer her up. A smile was now on her little face.

Colleen started the Volkswagen and backed out of the garage. The car was quite a bit older than her kids were, but it ran well most of the time. One of these days, she hoped they could afford a new car. She jumped out to close the garage door, got back in, fastened her seat belt, and turned on the heater.

"Let's sing!" Larry yelled.

"Okay. You don't have to yell, Larry. What do you want to sing?" The drive to his school was uneventful. They sang three songs on the way.

Then there was the school at last! With the car running, Colleen slipped out and, pushing the front seat forward, let Larry climb quickly to the pavement. She gave him a big kiss and hug. "Boys need hugs, too," she whispered in his tiny shell-shaped ear. He was still for exactly 5 seconds. Then off he ran, lunch box banging against his little leg. He seemed so tiny.

Once he was inside the door, Colleen slipped behind the steering wheel again. Looking in the mirror, she watched her baby girl waving out the window at the kids walking to school. She'd not had time to help Larry find his ball. She threw a tiny ping into the guilt bucket. Colleen wondered if working mothers ever got over the guilt.

"Okay, Emma, here we go to your school now. Just a little longer, and you'll be outside playing with the kids." Emma clapped her hands. She loved school.

"Mommy, hurry," she said.

Colleen drove the Volkswagen north about three blocks before she turned right and started uphill to pass over the freeway. She was starting to get her mind in order for the dilemma-du-jour at work. As she neared the top of the overpass, she felt the car chug once or twice. It grew silent as the engine stalled, and the car rolled slowly to a stop.

"Damn!" Colleen said under her breath. She was used to this. At times, the gas line of the little car popped off the pipe that sat at the top of the motor. It flew around the engine compartment in the back of the car, spewing gasoline all over and down into the street. Being used to it didn't make it easier. She would have to get out, open the little hood, find the hose, and stick it back on. Then she hoped that there would be enough gas left for the trip to the preschool and then finally to work.

She tried to ease the car over to the side with what little momentum was left. There wasn't enough. Her car was blocking traffic, and horns started honking immediately. Turning to the back seat, she said to Emma,

"Be a good girl for Mom and stay in your seat, okay? I just have to get out and check something in the back of the car. Okay? Emma, okay?"

"Okay, Mommy. I will be good." Emma was always good. Except, of course, when she wasn't.

Colleen found the little hose and reattached it to the engine. Her hands stunk of gasoline and were dirty to boot, but it couldn't be helped. As she rose from the engine compartment, a bus honked behind her. She nearly jumped out of her skin. When she whirled and frowned at the bus driver, she saw him gesturing at her. He wanted to push her out of the way.

"Okay!" Colleen called, slamming the little hood. She got back in the car, put it in neutral, and waited for the touch of the bus. They connected with a little nudge. Once the car started moving and separated from the bus, she tried to pop the clutch and start the car. It didn't start. She guided it to the side of the road and out of traffic's way. Once the lane cleared, she looked away from her mirror and down at the gas gauge. Empty.

Up ahead, at the bottom of the hill, there was a gas station. She felt her pocket. Yes, she had her plastic.

When everyone had passed her, Colleen got back out and stood between the car frame and the driver's side door. With her right hand on the steering wheel and her left on the front of the door frame, she started to push. It wasn't hard. The top of the overpass was flat and even, and she got the car going pretty well.

Then the road dipped downhill. The car started down. Colleen gasped as the steering wheel nearly slipped from her grasp. Continuing to build up speed, the little VW didn't need any more pushing. She'd let her mind wander, taking her eyes off the road.

"My life!" she whispered, thinking of her daughter in the backseat. Her arm was nearly torn from her shoulder as she clung to the steering wheel, running alongside. The wheels rotated faster. She ran harder, tears on her cheeks.

Many cars were stopped at the bottom of the hill, their brake lights sending a bright red warning. Beyond the cars, there was a six-lane boulevard, the busiest street in the whole city. Morning rush hour was just swinging into gear.

Panting and praying, hanging onto the steering wheel for dear life, Colleen ran and jumped, hoping she would not just slam into the side of the car. For a second, she was weightless. She pulled hard with her right arm. Then she slid miraculously into the driver's seat just as the car neared the entrance to the gas station. Foot hitting the brake, she jolted the car to a stop. The little VW rounded the corner into the lot.

Leaning her head against the steering wheel, Colleen breathed. She paused for a moment to think. She said a prayer of thanks. She counted a ton of pings going into the guilt bucket.

Once she had gained her composure, Colleen turned to the back seat. She'd have to apologize to her daughter. She was more than sorry. But there was little Emma, smiling and laughing, oblivious to the danger she had been in.

"Mommy! Let's go again, Mommy. I like it!" Colleen looked in amazement at her resilient little girl. What a doll. She wanted to pull her out of the car and hug her. "Mommy, the school now?"

Colleen turned to face the front of the car and the problem of the moment. She'd have to push the car up to the pump. Pretty sure she could handle this hurdle, she got out of the car on shaky legs. White-faced and careful, Colleen proceeded to do what Moms do every day -- just exactly what she had to do to keep things going.

Camping

Alex and Colleen took the kids camping in the Big Sur National Forest on the California coastline. It was a long drive and sticky with humidity. The traffic was easy, but the bends and twists in the road made it a hard drive in the little bug. Swaying back and forth in the backseat, Larry and Emma were irritable. Then Emma got carsick, and that put an end to any semblance of joy.

Alex generally drove carefully and safely, but this winding road brought out the beast in him. With the tent and all their gear on top of the car in a little luggage rack, Colleen worried they would capsize. At one curve, the sign read, "Slow to 15". Alex didn't slow down, and they nearly took a dive into the ocean. That was the alert he seemed to need to realize he needed to slow down.

They'd borrowed a big tent from Alex's mother. The tent, a cook stove, pans, dishes, and an ice chest were all strapped to the roof. Four sleeping bags were behind the back seat in the little storage space. Under the hood, which was the trunk of the VW, their clothes and towels were nestled. The kids couldn't wait to set up the tent and, as promised, to spend the night inside. Camping was a distant memory for Larry, but there was no memory for Emma. She had never even slept in a sleeping bag.

When they pulled up to the Ranger's hut to check in, they were told that there weren't many spots left….they should go right away and pick their campsite. Before children, Alex and Colleen had often camped under the trees on the edge of the campground. On this trip, those sites were all taken, and they had to pick a spot in the meadow. Once they chose one, it seemed different but not so bad. It would be easier to see the children, at least.

Alex and Colleen started to unload the car while Larry and Emma went to find the bathrooms. They set the camp stove and dish box on the table. Colleen pulled the sleeping bags out of the car and moved the ice chest to the back seat of the car, where they would lock it up before turning in. As Alex started to pull the tent down from the luggage carrier, he got very quiet. Ominously quiet. Colleen waited for him to speak. Finally, she said,

"Alex, what's wrong? You're so quiet." Alex looked at her sternly and cleared his throat.

"Damn it, Colleen," he said, "I forgot the tent poles!"

"What? How can we camp without tent poles?" Colleen asked, incredulous that he would forget something so basic.

"Well, we just will. We'll sleep out in the open as other people do."

"But what about bears?" Colleen's eyes were huge.

"Colleen, did you really think a tent would keep bears away? Come on. It'll be fine. I just have to tell the kids. They were so excited about the tent part." Alex turned his back and dipped his head, looking for something he'd dropped. Colleen had her kitchen chores to do and would leave the camp arrangements to Alex.

When Larry and Emma returned, Alex took them aside and told them about the tent poles. He had to explain to them what the poles were for and that the night would, unfortunately, not be spent inside a tent. Though both of his kids looked crestfallen, eight-year-old Larry worked up a smile and said,

"It's okay, Dad. The most important thing is that we're here. It'll be just a little more like real camping." Not wanting to ruin this mood by asking what "real camping" was, Alex instead smiled his relief. He enlisted the kids in setting up some sort of campsite. They laid the tent's canvas out on the ground and unrolled all the sleeping bags on top of it. It looked pretty silly, but at least the bottom of their sleeping bags wouldn't get damp.

"Alex, could you take the kids to the store and get us some firewood for tonight?" Colleen asked.

"No problem. I was just going to suggest that myself....we can take the long road up, and that way, they can see the whole campground."

"Do we get to walk?" Larry asked, very enthused.

"Yeah. We can walk if you help carry the wood back," Alex told him. "Get sweaters on, you guys. It's going to get chilly before we get back."

While they were gone, Colleen dragged the cooler out of the car, started dinner, and put some water on the camp stove to wash the dishes after they ate. The sun was already dipping in the west.

Alex, Larry, and Emma had been gone about 15 minutes when a car drove up to the campsite adjacent to theirs. A young man got out of the car and opened his trunk. He took out a brand spanking new tent in a box and set about putting it up in the middle of the campsite. Colleen watched him out of the corner of her eye. Next, he took out a camp stove in a box and assembled it on the picnic table. The last thing he fetched from his car was a lantern in a box. He spent a long time reading the instructions, and then, after installing a brand-new mantel, he set the lantern on the table and opened a beer.

Pretty soon, along came Alex and the kids. They were hungry from their walk and ready to eat. Colleen had the table set and sausages and potatoes cooking on the camp stove. She had set a pear on each of their plates. It was a good first-night meal. Alex started the fire so that it would have time to get going before they were ready to sit near it, and then they all sat at the table to eat. The kids ate like they were starved.

"Mommy, this is so good! Can I have more?" Emma asked. As Colleen got up to dish up seconds for her family, a car drove into the same campsite she had been watching earlier. This time she saw a woman with lots of blond hair leave the car. She was dressed in a

65

leather pantsuit. *For camping?* Colleen wondered. She gave everyone more sausages, potatoes, and onions and then sat down where she could watch her neighbors. She winked at Alex.

"What?" he said.

"Come sit by me," Colleen said. She moved over to make room for him. As he settled in next to her, she indicated the couple next door with a nod of her head. Then she leaned over and whispered in his ear,

"That man came in while you guys were gone. He was alone, and all his things were brand new, out of the box. Now this gorgeous blond comes in wearing a leather pantsuit. Could be better than TV." She smiled at Alex, and he nodded. They sat together sipping their wine while their neighbors, who were oblivious to the entire Big Sur experience, went about their camping like true novices.

Colleen got Larry busy doing the dishes and Emma drying them. Then she put away the food, stashing the cooler back in the car again. The neighbors were trying to light their camp stove and the lantern. She had a tiny cooler. It looked like they would try to cook their dinner in the dark. Colleen couldn't see any dishes or silverware.

Chuckling, she got the kids into their pajamas, and they all sat by the fire. They told a few stories and relaxed. The kids started nodding off within a half hour. She picked Emma up and carried her to her sleeping bag. Alex had placed the kids' bags in the middle and deposited Larry in the other center bag. Fresh air and good food, and they were out like lights.

Colleen and Alex took turns walking to the bathrooms to wash up and prepare for the night. When they were finished with the campsite shutdown, they sat again in their spots by their fire pit, watching the mysterious couple next door.

The young man had placed their tent in the middle of the meadow with no cover of trees or plants. The two of them sat at the picnic table until they were done eating and then carried their lantern into the tent. The whole tent became a lantern as they hung the light from the center post. Each movement of their silhouettes on the sides of the tent was visible to the entire campground. Alex and Colleen could hear them whispering and had trouble quieting their laughter. It was obvious that these two thought they were invisible.

They met in the tent's center, and their shadows got busy. Shadows of clothes dropped in every direction. Colleen leaned into Alex and whispered,

"Oh, my god! Why don't they shut off that terrible lantern? I feel incapable of turning away!" She was beside herself, trying to keep quiet. At long last, the couple settled into a low lump on the ground, and though the lantern blazed from the center post for a long time, the only thing Alex and Colleen saw was an oozing lump of shadow at the bottom of the tent.

Just before they gave it up for the night, putting out their fire and tossing the leftover wine into the bushes, they watched as the young, and obviously naked, camper next door stood up one last time and doused his lantern. Giggling and stumbling, Colleen and Alex went off to sleep a wonderful sleep under the stars, on top of their tent, in Big Sur National Forest, with their two sweet children between them.

The Hottest Summer Day

The end-of-summer days seemed longer and hotter than ever. Larry thought summer was boring in the new house. They didn't know any local kids, and he didn't like playing with his six-year-old sister Emma. The sun in this new town was intense. Wavy air hovered over the streets by mid-afternoon. The grass and trees were snappy dry, and the sky was a hazy grey. Larry's eyes were sore from keeping them open in the sun. Everyone was cranky lately because no one slept well in the new house. The floors and walls made strange and mysterious noises. It didn't feel like home at all.

Larry teased Emma to pass the time. Emma ran to their mother, crying about this torture just about every hour. To keep them occupied and apart, Colleen had given them each a job to do. Larry's job involved moving some lumber from one side of the garage to the other. It was mostly scrap -- a messy pile left by the previous owners. Emma had to clean the bathrooms. She was small and wiry but strong enough to do a good job. Her tiny limbs reached easily behind the toilets and into shower corners.

Larry whined as he worked. He hated being in the garage. He hated boring work, and he hated dirt. He hated being by himself the most. He wished Emma were nearby so he could harass her. He was very good at that. Even though it never made him happy to make her cry, he did it. He dragged the wood across the garage and threw it on the shelves. He wished he were done.

At the other end of the house, Emma was into her work. She scrubbed and wiped the floors and fixtures in the two bathrooms. This work was better than not doing anything. The water cooled her warm hands and arms. She sang little songs she had learned in kindergarten while she worked. The fresh smell of the cleanser filled the rooms.

Their mom was in the kitchen. She could hear Emma's sweet singing, and she smiled. She took the trash out to the garage and checked on Larry.

Lately, Larry always needed encouragement. It was so unlike him.

"How's it going, Larry?" she asked. "This is looking better every time I come out. Maybe you and Emma would like to play in the sprinkler when you're finished. What do you think?" Larry wasn't easily distracted from his misery. Still, he seemed to show a little interest in the sprinkler, although maybe he was just interested in getting another chance to annoy Emma.

"This is hard," Larry whined. "I keep getting cuts and slivers. Are you sure Dad wants this wood over there on those shelves? Maybe I should stop now, just in case." Colleen laughed and shook her head.

"Larry, if you worked instead of whining, you'd be done by now. I'm sure Dad will be pleased to find you've done a great job cleaning up this mess." She went back into the house and closed the door.

Larry sat down in the heat of the garage and cried. He was still a little boy even though everyone thought he was big. He was only nine on his last birthday. He shouldn't be treated like a handyman. He didn't want to work. He wanted to play, and he wanted his friends. He missed his old bedroom, the big tree in the yard, the picket fence he could see through, and the dog they had to leave behind. This new house was ugly. His new bedroom was dinky.

By now, Larry's face was covered with tear streaks and sweat trickles, which left vertical lines in the dirt on his cheeks. He'd used his forearm to push the sweat up and off his forehead so often that his hair stuck straight up in front. In short, Larry was a mess, just like the garage.

Head down and shoulders slumped, Larry got slowly to his feet and started hauling the wood again. He thought about how cool the sprinkler would feel. It just made him hotter. He hoped maybe he could finish before he fried to death out here in this dungeon. He thought about how much his mother would miss him if he died from crying in this musty, dark garage.

Spotting his wagon, he got an idea. He pulled the wagon over to the wood pile and filled it up. Then he pulled the wagon to the shelves and took the wood out. His idea was brilliant! Now he was getting somewhere!

Inside, Emma had finished the bathrooms. They sparkled and made her proud. After she washed the cleanser and germs off her hands and face, Colleen poured a glass of Kool-Aid for her and gave her a cookie. She sat at the kitchen table before the fan to eat it. Larry came in from the garage when she was almost finished with the treat. He was smiling!

"I've finished!" he crowed. "It was my super, great, spectacular idea that made it go so fast! I filled my wagon with wood and then used it to drag the wood to the shelves."

"Larry, that's amazing! What a wonderful idea!" Colleen said. She couldn't help smiling at his lined face and changed attitude. "Why don't you come in here and have some of these fresh cookies with Emma?"

Not needing to be asked twice, Larry raced toward the sink to wash his hands and face. As he passed the toaster, he saw his face and standing hair reflected on its side and started to laugh. Larry's chuckle was the most contagious laugh ever. Colleen and Emma started laughing with him, even though they had no idea why he was laughing.

"Look at me! I look like a mud man! And this hair—it's standing straight up in the air." Larry continued laughing as he made faces in the toaster. The laughter was making them all feel better.

71

While Larry and Emma ate their cookies, Colleen reached into her purse and found some change.

"You've both done such a nice job today that I'm going to give you each some money to spend: for Emma fifty cents and for Larry one dollar because he had to work outside in the heat." She put the money down on the table in front of her children. "Now, think about what you want to buy while you finish your cookies." Colleen left the kitchen and went to put the laundry in the dryer.

As soon as their mother left, Emma turned to Larry and said,

"Larry, let's put our money together and buy Mommy a present."

"Well, let me think about that," Larry replied. "Where could we go without getting in trouble, and what could we get her?" Emma was surprised that Larry seemed interested in shopping at all, especially in getting a present for someone besides himself. She thought hard.

"We could go to the little market that's on the way to our new school. We could ride our bikes. I'm sure they have something for this amount of money." Emma really had no concept of the amount of money she had, but it seemed like a lot to her.

"Owens Market, yeah, okay," Larry replied. "I'll go ask Mom. I'll tell her we're gonna ride our bikes to see if we cool off."

"Yippee! I'm so excited!" Emma got up and put their glasses in the sink. Larry left the room and was back in seconds.

"Mom said we can go! I'll get the money, and let's get out of here." Larry ran from the house into the garage. He pulled Emma's bike out to the driveway for her. He grabbed his own and wheeled it out, too. Together they climbed on the bikes and, starting slowly, they headed down the street to the market. The heat was still heavy on their backs, but the breeze they created by riding was very refreshing as it whipped up their arms and legs and whistled through their hair.

In front of the market, they tipped their bikes and set them on their sides on the sidewalk. Rushing through the old, thick glass door as it opened slowly inward, they envisioned a present sitting inside, waiting for them. There was, of course, no present waiting. They had to search the aisles, up and down, for just the right thing.

Owens Market was old, and the aisles were tight and dark. Food items, cleaning supplies, toiletries, and paper products were stacked very high, nearly to the caged light bulbs that cast so little light. Larry and Emma walked the aisles slowly, not wanting to miss anything. They knew that the right present was here. The money grew heavy in Larry's pocket—this was not as easy as they had thought it would be.

"How about some powder?" Emma asked. "Here's some powder in a little can."

"How much is it?" Larry wanted to know. He snatched it up and looked for a price. It was marked $2.15. "No, we don't have enough money for that. Let's take a look at this hairbrush. Oh, no! It's $4.00! I think we need to move to another part of the store, Emma."

Emma led the way to the aisle that bisected the store. Turning left, they could see the fresh fruits and vegetables crammed together in tiny cold cases at the far end of the store. Along the front edges of the coolers were old orange rubber hoses that the employees used to water the fresh produce every day. Without thinking, Larry reached for one of the hoses. The black swinging door at the back of the store slammed open, and the shop owner came through, heading directly towards them. Larry thrust his hand back into his pocket.

"Hello, children!" called Mr. Owens, the owner. "What brings you to my store today? Can I help you find something?" His bushy eyebrows raised behind the thick frames of his glasses. Emma reached for Larry's hand. Her little hand made him stand taller. The two of them leaned together, looking up the length of the striped apron to Mr. Owen's big, red face hovering over them.

"We're here to buy a present for our mother," Larry said, his head high. He hoped he looked honest. Even though he was, he doubted that Mr. Owens would think he was. Larry did not want his mother to know what they were up to. If Mr. Owens called her, it would ruin the surprise!

"Do you have any money with you?" Mr. Owens demanded. Larry's mouth fell open. He could not believe that Mr. Owens had asked such a stupid question.

"Yes, we do. Here – I'll show you." Larry pulled his hand from his pocket and spilled the $1.50 on the floor. He backed up, watched as the last nickel rolled, and stopped right by a little drain at the bottom of the cold case. Luckily nothing rolled into it. Larry started to feel threatened. He bit his lip. *I can't cry now,* he said to himself.

Emma leaned over to pick up the money. She and Larry had a little tug-of-war over her other hand which Larry held tightly in his own. She eventually won, broke free, and gathered up the money. Looking up at Mr. Owens, she told him,

"Mr. Owens, we have one dollar and fifty cents, and we want to surprise our mother with a present. We just don't know what to get her. Do you have any ideas?" Larry's mouth fell open. He thought for sure Mr. Owens would now throw them both out of the store. But to his surprise, Mr. Owens bent down to look into Emma's flushed face as he said,

"Let me see what I can help you find." He took Emma's hand and led her through the produce section. They stopped in front of the big cold watermelons. "Is your mother fond of watermelon? Is she as hot as everyone else today? Do you see a melon here that she might like?" The questions kept coming, and Larry thought he would never let Emma answer. Emma's eyes grew larger.

"My mother loves watermelon. I want to get her one of these!" Emma said. Mr. Owens reached into the pile and pulled a nice shiny dark green melon. He put it on a scale that hung from the

74

ceiling by three chains. The big dial bounced up and down, eventually registering 12 pounds.

"You have enough money for this one, little girl," he said. "Do you think you would like to get this for your mommy?"

"Oh, would I ever!" Emma said. She turned to Larry with questioning eyes. "What do you think, Larry? Do you think Mom would love this nice cool melon?"

What could Larry say? His mouth was watering. He pictured a knife slipping smoothly along that green skin before slipping in with a tiny "pop" and then the cold, pink juice slowly dripping out onto the kitchen counter. So it was agreed that the watermelon would be the present they would buy for their mother. Mr. Owens took the melon to the front of the store and rang up their purchase on his cash register. The big buttons slid down the long slots, and the drawer popped open with a ringing and a clatter. In the window at the top, Larry and Emma could see the total – 96 cents! They would get change!

Mr. Owens counted back the change from the dollar into Larry's hand. Four pennies to add to the 50 cents left in his pocket. He and Emma would divide that up later. Then Mr. Owens took the watermelon from the counter and lowered it into Larry's hands.

Larry's eyes nearly slipped from their sockets. The melon was heavy! He struggled not to drop it. He wanted to be Emma's hero but was unsure he could do it! Walking carefully to the door, he stepped on the rubber mat. The door swung slowly open. He walked to his bike and asked Emma if she could lift it from the sidewalk.

Emma struggled with the bike. It was big and seemed much heavier than her own. But she finally got it up and held it for Larry. He let the melon lead him to the bike and leaned it against the handlebars. He had no basket. He couldn't let go of the melon. He couldn't possibly get his leg over the center bar. He would have to walk, balancing the melon against his handlebars.

And so they started out for home. Emma led with her little bike, and Larry followed with his big red bike leaning against his body, the melon rocking on the handlebars and banging against his chest. After two blocks, Larry stopped. His scalp was wet, and drops had started to run down his cheeks. His hands were slick with sweat.

"Emma," he said, "I can't walk this home. It's too hot and too far. The melon keeps slipping, and I'll probably drop my bike if I keep going like this! Do you think you could ride home and get Mom to bring the car?"

He knew Emma would have to be courageous to ride home alone. She might get lost or just be afraid, but they had no choice. Either Emma went or Larry went, and Larry would not leave Emma there alone. He waited for her decision. Looking up at him with big eyes, Emma said,

"Okay, Larry! I'll ride like the wind." She hopped on her bike and left him in the dust. When next he looked up, Emma was a block away, and her feet were a blur of motion.

Emma rounded the corner and sped up the driveway at home. She ran to the front door and rang the bell. Colleen came to answer the door and looked out over Emma's head.

"Where's Larry?" she asked Emma.

"Mom, come quick. Bring the car and come get Larry." A look of concern crossed Colleen's face. Her forehead wrinkled up, and she looked into Emma's eyes.

"Where IS Larry, Emma? Is he hurt?"

"No, Mom. He just needs help getting home." Emma was trying to think of ways to ask her mother to pick up Larry without telling her what Larry was doing. But Colleen was not budging. Emma waited.

"Please, Mommy, come get Larry. We bought you a surprise, and now Larry needs help. Please, Mommy!" Finally, Colleen stood up and went back into the house.

"Come in, Emma, and close the door. I'm going to have to find my keys and glasses before I can go." Emma followed her mother from room to room as she searched for her glasses. She always set them down somewhere and forgot where they were. Suddenly Emma burst out laughing. She bent at the waist and nearly fell over. She laughed so hard that Colleen whirled around and looked at Emma's little red face.

"What's going on, Emma? What's so funny?" she asked. Gasping, Emma looked up at her mother and squeaked,

"Larry looked so funny standing there in the hot sun with that great big watermelon, trying to hold up his bike!" Even as the words left her lips, Emma knew she could not call them back. She knew she had said something she shouldn't have. "Oh, no! Don't tell Larry I told. Please don't tell him. He was so excited about the surprise!"

Colleen stopped hunting and looked at Emma with a smile.

"Come on, Emma. Let's go get your brother." She headed out the back door to the Volkswagen that stood in the driveway.

They drove up the street until they found Larry by the side of the road with the huge watermelon balanced on the handlebars of his bike. He was white with the effort it took to keep the melon from slipping to the ground. Sweat was dripping down his poor face like a waterfall. Colleen got out of the car and hugged Larry. She lifted the watermelon from his arms.

"Is this for me?" she asked. "This is the best present ever. It's just what I wanted on this very hot day." Turning around, she found Emma behind her and gave her a kiss. "You two are my treasures. Thank you for thinking of me!"

Larry and Emma both turned beet red as they were praised. They shuffled their feet and wondered what to do next. Colleen told Larry he would have to ride his bike home—there was not enough room in the car. She pushed her seat forward and set the melon in the back seat. Then she and Emma climbed in the car, and they all headed home to pop the skin of that shiny green melon and sink their teeth into the delicious juicy pink fruit.

Weekend Away

Alex and Colleen stuffed the little trunk of the VW with two suitcases and the backseat with their two kids. In minutes they were off for a long-planned weekend in San Diego. The kids loved the hotel because of the pool, the balcony, and the Coke machine. Alex and Colleen just loved getting away and, in the case of San Diego, sitting by the deep blue pool and having drinks with umbrellas brought to their chairs by tanned waiters in colorful Hawaiian shirts.

The sun was shining, with no smog in sight. Even for Southern California, it was a miraculously beautiful day. As they pulled onto the freeway heading south, Colleen looked over at Alex and said,

"Two miles...feel any different?" Alex smiled and winked. It was an old joke between them. On every trip they took, they counted the distance from home and celebrated how good they felt with each passing mile.

So far, Emma and Larry had been good, but of course, they were only two miles from home. Colleen tried not to anticipate trouble, but the hour and a half they had to drive would probably not be spent in pure peace. She leaned her head back and watched as the scenery passed by.

Alex popped a CD in the slot, and he and Colleen hummed his chosen tunes. Elton John sang "Daniel" as Colleen smiled and rolled her window down. A cool breeze slipped in and took her hair for a ride. It felt miraculous. The sun was warm on her right arm, face, and chest. Oh, if only every day were filled with this much of a sensory menu.

The miles clicked by. Larry was busy with the directions for his new camera. Emma was daydreaming, her little feet not quite reaching the floor.

"Dad," Larry called to his father, "the basketball playoffs are this weekend. The Lakers play tomorrow. Can we watch the game in our room?" Colleen rolled her eyes. She had wanted it to be a family weekend, not a weekend of sitting in front of the TV. Alex looked at her and back at the road.

"I forgot they were on this weekend," he told her quietly, "I'm sorry." He called back to his son, "We couldn't possibly miss the Lakers game no matter where we are, Larry." Turning again to Colleen, he said, "I'll make it up to you, honey. We'll go somewhere nice next weekend if you want—just you and me." He continued sweet-talking Colleen until she finally blushed with his suggestions and agreed that he could indeed make it up to her with at least one of his ideas.

"Okay, you win, boys. My worry is what Emma and I will do tomorrow while you're engrossed in your ball game. I guess something will come to me."

Larry put down his camera and started slamming his baseball into his mitt. Emma spoke as if she had missed the entire exchange.

"Mom, did you bring my pink bathing suit? I want to go swimming as soon as we get there. I hate that ugly orange suit – it makes me feel like a little kid." Colleen had trouble not laughing. Emma was, after all, still a little kid—she was only 8.

"Honey, I brought both of your bathing suits just in case you might need them both. When one is wet, you might not want to put it back on right then. The orange one looks cute on you. What don't you like about it?"

"Mommy! I hate that little skirt around the bottom. You know it looks silly. I should be wearing a little bikini or something like that."

Alex was suddenly interested in this conversation. He raised his eyebrows and, looking in the rearview mirror, he said,

"Emma! There will be no wearing of bikinis until you are much older---like 16 or something. Right, Colleen? Maybe even 18."

Colleen sometimes regretted how small their car was. When one of her kids started wailing, she could not get away from the volume.

"Emma, it's okay. Daddy's just kidding. You can wear a bikini very soon," Colleen soothed. "Calm down now and dry your eyes before you leak on Larry."

The air was hot, but at least it was stirring as the car moved through it. As he gazed out the window, Larry's baseball continued to whack in the palm of his glove, annoying even Colleen. Eventually, Emma started to fidget.

"It's too hot back here," she whined. "Larry's making too much noise! He smells bad. Oh no, he touched me!!!" Her alarm rate went up with the miles. Colleen tried to calm her kids, to keep them happy, but the back seat was just so small and cramped. There was no escaping one's sibling in such a space as this.

Eventually, the exit sign for Hotel Circle appeared up ahead. Alex slowed and left the freeway. When the hotel sign appeared in the sky, everyone in the car sat up and smiled. Soon they would be getting out of the tiny car.

The evening passed uneventfully with a delicious steak dinner and an evening swim. As the temperature cooled and the shadows lengthened, Alex and Colleen put the kids to bed and enjoyed a cocktail on their balcony. They were content sitting just outside their room with their feet up and a breeze blowing on their sun-blushed skin.

In the morning, the family went to breakfast by the pool, where they chose from a buffet of fruits, rolls, and muffins. The coffee was good—rich, dark, and steamy hot. With birds singing as they ate and the sun passing through the trees, making patterns on the walkways, the family was at peace.

Colleen perused the paper for ideas. She wanted to make it a special day for her daughter. "Emma, do you want to go to the zoo today?"

"Mom, we've done that so many times."

"Well, okay, how about a walk at the beach? Or we could just wander around at Balboa Park. On weekends they have clowns and mimes, musicians, and craftspeople. Does that sound fun to you?"

"No, not really. The beach will be hot and dirty, and the park will be crowded. Why don't we just go shopping?" Ah, shopping! Emma's new interest! The little girl was learning that money was fun to spend. Alex lifted his eyebrows as he looked at Colleen as if to say, "*What are you raising here?*"

Colleen finally gave in. She didn't mind shopping; it wasn't something she would normally do on her weekend away from home. But the mall was very close, and she and Emma were footloose. So they agreed to shop after a quick swim.

By the time their bathing suits were hung in the shower, and Emma and Colleen were back in shorts, Alex and Larry had the TV on and were searching channels for the ball game they wanted to watch. Grabbing the keys, Colleen leaned in to kiss Alex, but he didn't even seem to notice her. She laughed and rolled her eyes at Emma, which made Emma feel like Colleen's friend, not her daughter. She liked that. Out they went, swinging their purses. As they made their way down the stairs to the car, they could hear the ball game echoing from other rooms as well as from the pool bar.

They drove just around the corner and then just a few blocks to the mall. The parking lot was stifling, heat wafting up from the blacktop. Walking into the air-conditioned space was a relief. It was bright and noisy in the wide aisles of the mall. Voices echoed from floor to floor as shoppers called out to their children and to one another. Speakers played music they thought they recognized, but on second thought, they weren't sure.

They window-shopped for an hour or more. When they got to the food court, they decided it was time to eat lunch.

Colleen was proud of Emma. She hadn't asked for one thing all morning. After lunch, she intended to shop for Emma's school clothes. They watched the other diners and compared their impressions, something they often did when they were out to eat. There were a lot of babies in the dining area. Emma eyed them and sat up taller.

"There sure are a lot of little kids here, Mom. Do you think we might have another baby in our house someday?"

"Where did that come from?" Colleen wondered. Turning to the sweet child she had mothered, Colleen said, "No, Emma. I don't think another child will ever come to live in our house. We have you, and we have Larry…that's all we ever wanted." Emma seemed relieved. Making space for a baby would really cramp her style.

"Well, if you're about done, we can go to Penney's now," Colleen said. Emma got up and threw away their trash, and stacked their trays on the pile nearby. Colleen put her purse over her shoulder, and they went off to J C Penney.

As they entered the store on the second floor, Colleen was assaulted with signs for a linen sale. She couldn't pass it up. Linens were a weakness. She held Emma's hand and escaped into the aisles of sheets and towels. Colleen was dragging, but she knew she couldn't take a nap anyway, as long as that game was on TV in their room. Turning a corner, they suddenly came upon a huge bin of pillows. They looked so inviting to her tired eyes.

"Emma, look. Two for the price of one! We could get pillows for everyone, and it would only cost the price of two pillows!" Emma did not share her mother's enthusiasm. She just looked at the pillows blankly and wandered off.

Colleen decided Emma was right. Besides, she had promised school clothes and then stopped for linens. They went to the girls' department and got some T-shirts, a pair of jeans, a nice little sweater, and some socks for Emma for school. They gathered the packages and returned toward the store's exit into the mall corridor.

They passed by the linens again. Colleen couldn't help herself. She pulled on Emma's shirt sleeve and headed for the pillows. She selected two King size pillows and two regular pillows. They were so big, white, soft, and clean. In line, she whipped out her Penney's card. In a matter of minutes, the pillows were theirs. The clerk put the pillows in two big grey shopping bags to ease the burden of carrying the four pillows.

Somehow they made their way down the mall with the two big bags and Emma's two little bags. They bumped into a few people, but most could see they were overloaded, so they understood and smiled at their progress.

As they walked through the mall exit door, Colleen caught sight of her little Volkswagen sitting in the parking lot under a palm tree. Her smile drifted away. She had forgotten how little their car was and that they had barely managed to fit into it the day before. Her dilemma would now be to fit those same four people, two suitcases, and four large pillows into the little VW. She stopped and stared at her beloved car.

Emma turned around when she felt her mother stop.

"Mom, what are you doing? Come on!" She saw the look on her mother's face. She swiveled back to the car, then to her mom, then back to the car again. Her face also changed.

"Mom! Where are you going to put those huge pillows?" she demanded.

Colleen unlocked the car door and pushed the pillows into the backseat. They popped back at her. She pushed them back in. The big plastic bags bloated out the door. Colleen used the ignition key to stab one of the clear plastic bags surrounding each pillow. It

84

popped with a loud sound. She then popped the other three bags. Pow! Pow! Pow! She shoved the pillows in again.

"Emma," she said, turning around.

"Mom?" Emma answered. Their eyes met. In unison, they looked over at the car. The pillows bulged out the windows. Emma giggled. The situation seemed impossible. "We could return the pillows," Emma said.

"But I want these pillows," Colleen answered. "I want them really bad." Colleen turned her back. When she turned back around, the pillows were still sticking out the car's windows. The sight was funny, really. She could see that. But she really did want to take the pillows home.

"Emma, do you remember a watermelon event we experienced together? Maybe you don't. It was awhile back. Oh, my god, why did I buy those stupid pillows?" Colleen asked no one in particular. "What am I going to tell Alex?"

"How are we going to get them home?" Emma countered.

"How are WE going to get home is more to the point," Colleen answered. "This time, Larry can't just ride his bike home!" The dilemma suddenly seemed very funny to them. They were both dissolved in laughter.

But when they returned to the hotel, they saw the faces of Alex and Larry, who had watched their team go down to defeat. They thought better of laughing in their presence.

By intuition, both Emma and Colleen knew not to talk about the pillow incident. They didn't want to ruin the rest of the weekend. Over the course of the evening, one of them would smirk or giggle, but in time, they seemed to forget the story altogether.

Then Sunday came. It was noon, and time to pack the car. Bearing suitcases, plastic bags full of wet bathing suits, and a bag of doughnuts, the family members walked toward the VW, talking and

85

happy. The back windows were filled with white. It was the first time Larry and Alex had seen the car in two days. It appeared to be stuffed to its limit with clouds. Larry looked over at his father and said,

"Dad, what's wrong with our car?" Emma let out a loud snort, and Colleen looked up, surprised to see the pillows pressed against the windows. She realized then that she'd simply forgotten about them. She wasn't sure what to say, but huge gales of laughter were pushing up inside her. When her eyes met Emma's, she could not hold back any longer. She and her daughter started laughing, choking, and gasping. Alex looked at her as if she were losing her mind. Colleen finally was able to tell the story of how they'd purchased the pillows and stuffed them into the car when they went shopping.

"I should have told you then, but you were both so upset about losing your ballgame that I just couldn't. And they were such a great bargain! And then, well, then I just forgot."

"Mom! You forgot? How could you forget?" Larry asked her. "Where are Emma and I supposed to sit?" Larry was indignant. "We aren't so little anymore, you know!"

A bewildered Alex opened the car door, and pillows sprung out, smashing him in the face. He looked over at Colleen, and she sputtered but could not stop laughing. Alex tried to look stern. He couldn't. He smiled. Then he laughed. Then he couldn't stop. Larry and Emma looked amazed.

"Where have you put our real parents?" Larry wanted to know. Standing in the hotel's parking lot with bags and suitcases strewn at their feet, the family succumbed to the ridiculous. A solution had to be found, but the absurdity of the day consumed them first.

Finally, the pillows were removed from the individual plastic bags and the grey shopping bags. The king-sized pillows were smashed together in the middle of the seat so that Larry and Emma could sit on either side of them, each by a window. Though

86

it required that the brother and sister be jammed against the windows, at least they did not have to touch each other as the car moved. Emma and Larry sat on the two remaining pillows. It was the only solution.

Riding home surrounded by pillows was like resting in a marshmallow dream. Luckily they slept most of the way, and there was no complaining about Larry touching Emma or Emma touching Larry. A kind of euphoria set in.

As the years went by, the sight of a fluffy white pillow would sometimes set the family to laughing, sometimes in very awkward situations, but there was nothing to be done about it. The memory of that day was one they shared many times. And though a lesson was relearned about compulsive buying and its consequence, it was evident that said lesson had to be learned again and again over the years, frequently accompanied by laughter and the mental picture of pillows smashed against the windows of a very small car or a boy and a watermelon by the side of the road.

Long Lost Child

I returned from the mailbox, planning to sit at the kitchen table and look through the stack of mail I'd carried in. My kitchen was quiet with the family out to work or school. My dog, who had run to the mailman for a cookie just moments before, now napped under my favorite chair, his purple rubber ball only 6 inches from his wee nose.

A beautiful view lies just out the kitchen window — a sloping hill covered in lawns and flowers in rows. Above the table hangs a copper lamp from my father's house. It reminds me of his strong, capable hands and bushy eyebrows over those clear blue eyes. I had spread a tablecloth of blue and white checks with embroidery around the edge. Centered on it stood a bright orange vase filled with yellow flowers from my garden.

I'd poured a cup of coffee when I came in. Now I took my usual seat at the table. I set the cup on the table next to the pile of mail. A breeze was blowing in from the flower beds. It carried the scent of all those blossoms just outside. I felt at peace. Now and then, I just fell in love with my life all over again. It was that kind of day.

I shuffled through the mail: a couple of bills, some flyers for real estate or cable TV, a little newspaper full of local ads, a birthday card for a daughter who will turn 11 this Saturday, and a few requests from local charities. Stuffed in the middle of the stack was an envelope postmarked from Colorado Springs. I didn't recognize the return address. It was handwritten. I imagined it from another charity asking me to donate to their cause. I set it down and considered it. Took a drink of my coffee. Picked up the envelope again. My curiosity was aroused.

When I opened the envelope, a photo fell out of a folded letter. I picked it up and looked at it. The young man in the photo had a familiar face, but I couldn't place him. I opened the letter and sat forward to read it.

Two sentences in, I started to shake. The paper wouldn't be still, so I placed it on the table, the better to read it. Though my head blocked the lamp's light as I bent forward, I didn't notice.

I put the letter down and fell back in my chair. I picked up the picture again and studied it. I reached into the pocket of my sweater for a tissue. I was sure it was there — I remembered stuffing it there earlier. I looked out the window and wiped the tears off my cheeks. Gazing out the window, I saw the sky. It was like I had never seen it before. It was so so blue! It spread so far that it seemed to have no end.

A bell rang on the stove. My pie was done, and I had forgotten it. I don't know how long I'd been looking out the window. At last I jumped up and, taking a towel from the drawer, I used it to lift the pie from the oven. I set the hot dish on a trivet, lowered my head and smelled the pie. It was heaven.

I went back to the table. My coffee had gone cold. I refilled the cup and warmed it in the microwave. I settled down at the table and picked up the letter once more. I took a deep breath. Okay, I said, I am okay. I wished someone were there with me, but I didn't really want anyone. This letter was long expected and only by me. I didn't really want to share it with anyone because no one would understand. Maybe ever.

"Dear Rita," the letter said. "I believe you may be my birth mother. I have looked for you for a very long time."

My child! I have looked for you since I was 15 years old! I am so happy you have found me. I am so happy! I got up from the table and went to the window just to look out and see the world and its never-ending mystery.

I knew what my life had become. I loved my life, this life. But for years, I'd missed my son. I had worried about him, dreamt of him, and wished for this day. I'd missed this person whose name is… I had to go back to the envelope to find his name. His name was perfect. His name was Patrick. I wiped more tears from my face. He had always been Patrick. Even when he was born, someone somewhere had a name already chosen for him. It was Patrick.

I sat down again and picked up the letter. It was short since he wasn't even sure I was the proper person to address it to. It said he wanted to be in contact if that would suit me, and he would be happy to fly out and meet me for coffee, staying only as long as there was goodwill between us. I was overjoyed! I was petrified. I was mystified. I had dreamt of this day, but I had never gotten very far in imagining it. I couldn't—I didn't have a face to put on the man who would say these words to me. And now, here he was.

I had to think. There was so much baggage involved in this. It wasn't just me, and it, more than likely, would not be just *MY* decision. And then, of course, he wasn't a baby anymore—he was a man who grew up knowing nothing about me or how I would feel about anything. I put my coffee cup in the sink. I put my face to the pie again and inhaled its delightful fragrance. I went out and left the door wide open.

I walked through the flowers. I had never seen such color, each petal, each stem, the leaves, the bees. I was overwhelmed with the experience of seeing, breathing, of living! I took that picture out of my pocket again and looked at it. "Patrick," I said. "Hello, Patrick!" I laughed, and I felt those tears again. I sat in the middle of those flowers and stared at my son's picture.

Naturally, I am a list maker, but this didn't feel like a situation for making a list. I had to go with my heart on this. My head was spinning, and hours were slipping by. I reread that letter until it nearly turned to tissue. He was, I knew, 24. Now I also knew that he was just finishing college, that he was happy and had a happy life with very caring and special parents. He was handsome! That was all I knew, but it felt like more than my head could comprehend.

I saw the little red car before I heard it. I looked up, and there it was. My beloved husband in his blazing red car, the man who had seen me through adulthood thus far. He was kind and wholesome and cared for our daughter and me. He kept our yard so gorgeous I could not think of one thing more we could add to make it perfect. And here he was, home. In a way, I didn't want to share this feeling with anyone. I was sitting on the flowerbed! I had made a pie, and that was it for the entire day. I waved. I loved him. What would he think?

Les parked, came over to the yard, and squatted near me.

"What's up?" he said. "Are you okay?" He helped me up, and I said, "Could we just sit in the yard for awhile, please?" So we did. We walked to the patio and pulled chairs close together along the edge of the cement, where we sat side by side, our forearms touching. We sat until the sky turned pink, until the shadows were long, until the morning glories closed up for the night, and a tiny piece of the moon appeared in the sky.

"Stay here," I said. "I'll go get us a drink and something to nibble." Les had his shoes off and his toes in the grass. His shirt was unbuttoned at the neck. He was relaxed and happy, I think. When I came back, the letter was in my pocket. I pulled up a couple of little tables, and we set a bottle of wine on one with two glasses and popcorn and a cut-up apple on the other. We toasted and drank. Les is so patient. He knew not to rush me, and he didn't. I can't be like that, but I am glad he can.

"Les," I said, looking toward him, "I love you with all my heart." Poor Les looked worried. I touched his arm. "I got a letter today. It's a big deal. I have spent the entire day thinking about it. I guess it's time to share." I pulled out the letter and handed it to him. Les had known about my teenage pregnancy since we first were a couple, telling each other everything in our hearts. It had never come up again. I held it close all these years, but we did not discuss it. Ever again, for whatever reason. It just didn't come up.

The letter unfolded. Les breathed deeply and started to read. His back seemed to relax. He read it again. I waited.

"How do you feel about this?" he asked me finally. He asked ME! All day I had thought about it. All day I had thought about it. All day. Did I know how I felt? My question was, how did he feel? Nothing seemed more important.

"I feel so many things I can't even begin to tell you," I said. I was just bursting to talk, so I did. "I feel happy he is happy. I feel happy he's had a good family and a good life. I feel apprehensive. I feel excited. I feel relieved! I feel overjoyed that he wants to include me in his life in some small way. I feel small, and then I feel expansive. Everything feels changed and beautiful, but there is fear there, too.

"I also feel the way this goes is a family decision. I have had all day to think about this, but you have not. Do you need time to consider this? Do you want to share how you feel right now? Do you want to sit here and think while I whip up some dinner?"

Les laughed. He is amazing. He is considerate and wise. "Stop!" he said, laughing. "I like the idea of a few minutes to digest, so why don't you go make dinner and call me when it's ready?"

Secretly that was what I'd hoped for. Selfishly I wanted more time to myself to think and to dream. But really, I did not want him to give me an immediate answer. I wanted it to be a considered answer. And just in case he had a negative reaction, I could do with a few more minutes of hope before I heard about it. He probably already knew how this would make him feel and may have thought of it repeatedly for years, but I wanted him to think about it even more now that it was real. I was not hoping for a gut reaction but rather a thoughtful opinion. So I got up and went inside.

Our daughter Jane had swimming practice after school, and I knew she would be late. I was glad to have this time to get Les used to the idea before I had to tell her about it. This was her only sibling, and she didn't even know he existed. It would be a wow moment. I stood at the window and watched the last sun dip below the horizon before I broke the spell and got busy with dinner. I knew

93

how lucky I was to have this view every day. I really did love my life. Was trouble stirring? Did I welcome change or fear it? I had no idea.

Without me even noticing, everything had already changed.

I whisked, baked, and boiled, moving around in my kitchen just like always. Except for this day, I was one minute laughing, one-minute crying, and the next minute shaking and dropping things. At last, it was ready. "Dinner, Les!" I called out the window.

He came in then, his shoes in hand, his hair mushed up like it is when he's been rubbing his head, trying to figure something out. He looked like the man I loved. I hugged him, and we sat down. Filled our plates. Picked up our forks.

"So, Rita, first of all, I'd like to remind you that this is a real person we're talking about here. He has feelings and thoughts that may not be in line with yours. He may be very different from you and me and Jane, very different from our family. And yet, once we contact him, he will be our family, won't he? Different or similar, he will be part of us once you say yes. And he won't just suddenly not be there if you decide he's not what you wished for. He's not going to disappear if you change your mind."

"I know," I said. "And he will be a stranger, too, an adult! He won't be a baby or some little kid we can move around at our whim. I have thought about that today. Quite a bit, in fact."

"You might not love him. You might not even like him. He could be peculiar or mean. Have you thought about that?"

"I know. That's what makes me frightened of this. When he left my life, he was a blank slate. He was a faceless, nameless baby to me. Now he is someone. Someone I don't know!"

Les put his fork on the table and took a long drink of water. He reached for my hand. "Rita," he said, "I want you to be happy. I want you to have everything. I want all your dreams to come true! But just this once, let's not be hasty to decide which way to go with

94

this, okay? Let's talk to Jane. Let's consider all things and be sure of our response before we blurt it out and then regret it. What do you think?"

"You are my anchor, Les. I trust your judgment, and I want to do things right. I think you hit the nail on the head. I have thought about this all day and feel just about what you do. I'd like to talk to Jane tomorrow, but not tonight. I'm not sure I'm ready to talk to her about it, but I'd like to wait until I am surer how I feel. I don't want to risk her feelings for me, either. So much is involved in this decision. I could not live if she stopped loving me as she does.

"Then there is that other part of me that wants to call Patrick right now! It's so hard to wait, but I've waited a long time already. When I think of him, he is a stranger. He is my son. It's an enigma."

Holding hands, we looked at each other. It was the right thing to do, and we both knew it. Jane first. She was our daughter. All these years, she had been my daughter, our daughter. She didn't just drop in. She had to come first.

That night I woke to nightmares. I woke hollering and kicking. Les woke me and held me. I cried and told him about when I had Patrick and how hard it was for me to give him up, how it was thrust on me, not as my decision, but as a choice without an alternative. It felt like part of me was cut away and torn from my body.

I tried to sleep after that, but it would not happen. I was, first of all, afraid of more nightmares, but I was mostly too wound up. I got up and had a cup of chamomile tea. I put honey in it, lots of honey. I took a paper and pen and tried to think how to tell Jane. I took a few notes and started yawning. I went back to bed and fell sound asleep—no more dreams.

Jane is at a judgmental age. She is a kind person and has immense sweetness. But she doesn't have patience for mistakes, especially stupid ones. I wasn't sure how she would react to her mother making the very hard decision I'd had to make, which felt like my only choice then. I didn't want to alienate her, and I didn't

95

want her to ask me not to call Patrick because she thought I was a bad person or because my mistake in giving him up was unforgivable. Or even because her first reaction was jealousy.

I wanted to be patient and wait to tell her until I was more prepared, but as luck would have it, she found my notes on the table when she got up.

"Hey, Mom, what's this about?" she asked, holding the papers aloft. "My name's at the top! Did I do something wrong?"

Bold move. I asked her what she wanted for breakfast!

"Come on, Mom, just tell me. Is there a problem? What did I do?"

I poured her a glass of juice and told her to sit down. I turned my back to get some coffee and to breathe for a minute. She read me.

"Mom? Are you avoiding me?"

"No, Jane, I am not avoiding you, and no, you did nothing wrong. I have to talk to you about something, and I am trying to think how to do it." I held up my hand to silence her. "Just bear with me, Jane. All in good time. Sit." She sat. I sat. I needed worry beads, but since I don't have any, I just had to try to still my hands.

"When I was 14, just three years older than you are now, I had this friend who had this friend. She introduced me to her friend, and I loved him instantly. I wanted never to be apart from him. My friend smiled when she saw us together. She told me she knew we'd be a good match. And she seemed right about that. We were nuts about each other. We had the same friends, went to the same school, and had the same sense of humor. We were both studious, and our dads were both hard workers, our moms loving and kind.

"After a few months, we started to hang out at his house after school, and then when school let out in June, we spent even more time there. His mom worked, but we were just friends. Our parents never blinked. At first, we played video games or CDs. We sang together, watched movies, played with his dog, ate chips, and drank sodas. Then one day, we banged into each other in the hall and ended up kissing. It was unexpected but not unwelcome. It just seemed inevitable.

"Nothing more happened for awhile. We held hands, and we became an item. One day I fought with my mom. I came over crying, and he held me while I cried. That day more happened."

"Ew, Mom, don't tell me! Please spare me!" Jane made a horrible face. She seemed ready to leave the room, so I had to hold her hand to keep her involved in my story, which, even to me, was getting pretty long!

"Okay, I'll skip some details, alright?" She nodded. "To make a very long story short, we ended up having sex before the end of summer. It was very childish in my memory, but it felt so grown up to me then. I tried to refuse, but it got harder and harder to say no because I liked it! I know, TMI.

"Well, anyway, he broke up with me when school started. I don't really remember why. I think his dad got transferred or something. I don't really remember seeing him after that. I was heartbroken. Devastated. He was my everything. I was surrounded by memories of him and constantly bursting into tears."

"Wow, that's a sad story, Mom. You never told me that before. I'm sorry."

"Well, Jane, there's more. It's all sad. By Thanksgiving, I had not had my period, and I was getting really worried. I talked to my best friend, and she was really no help, but she did feel bad for me. Finally, I had to go to my mom. She was livid! Not understanding at all! I thought she might be kind to me, but she wasn't. I think she slapped me. Or I might have imagined that. Anyway, she took me to her doctor, and sure enough, I was pregnant. Now my heart really broke."

"Mom! How horrible for you! What did you do then?" I was so pleased Jane was not judging me badly. I had worried she would holler for me to shut up or just bounce out of the room. She was so mature in the way she handled this revelation! But wait. Maybe she hadn't thought it through?

"Well, my parents would not allow abortion, and I probably would not have had one even if I had wanted to be done with this situation. It was HIS baby, after all! And besides, I was 15! I needed my parents for everything, which seemed to include thinking! So I kept going to school until everyone could tell I was pregnant. I was just a sophomore! So young. It was a scandal. Eventually, I quit going to school and just hung out at home studying.

"By spring, my baby was due." I looked at Jane, and her eyes were very wide. She was pale and did not blink or show any emotion. She appeared literally spellbound. I went to a few classes to learn how to have a baby, and then one night, I had these tremendous wrenching pains, and Mom and Dad took me to the hospital. The pains continued until morning and were worse than anything I had imagined. Finally, they said I was ready, and off I went to be delivered.

"I never saw my baby. I knew it was a boy because they said that in the delivery room. He left the room before I did. Off to his new family and the arms of his new mother. I had to go home in two days, heal up, and finally return to school, ashamed and sad."

"Grandma and Grandpa made you do that? They took away your baby? I can't believe they were so mean!"

"Oh, no, Jane. You shouldn't feel that way. When I was going through it, I did think it was cruel that I had to let my baby go, but over the years, I have realized that what they did was the best for the baby and me. He needed stability in his life, not a teenage mother! And I needed to keep becoming the person I was destined to be. They did what they thought best, which was just how it was back then. I was just a little girl and couldn't take care of him and go to school myself. My boyfriend had left, so I had no one on my side. I just let him go. I had no choice." Suddenly I started to cry, and Jane got up and came to hug me and comfort me.

"Mom, don't cry, Mom! It was all a long time ago. What do you think happened to him, that baby boy?"

I wiped my eyes and took Jane's hand in mine. I love this little girl so much! I would never have told her the story of my pregnancy if it weren't for Patrick — because of him showing up and forcing me to tell her. For just that one minute, I hated him for putting me in this position. I sat up straighter and looked her in the eye.

"That baby grew up in Colorado. He wrote me a letter which I got yesterday. His name is Patrick. He wants to make contact with me and stay in touch. He's 24 years old. He's your brother, Jane. It's a lot to consider all at once, but I wanted to be upfront with you about this entire thing. I value your opinion. You are level-headed and kind. Can you tell me what you think?"

"Oh my god! I have a brother?" I nodded. She stood up and stared at me. No blinking, no frown. A tear ran down her cheek.

"I guess when you were talking, I didn't think of this story as having a present tense! Thank you for telling the truth. I guess I am pretty curious. I might like to meet him. I think I would. Did you talk to Dad about it?"

"Well," I said, "the letter just came yesterday, and your dad and I talked about it once he got home from work, but we haven't talked much about it—just some. We did, however, decide it was a family decision because it involved all of us. And I don't want to get together with Patrick only to reject him because it's inconvenient or upsetting. He is a real person with thoughts and feelings that we know nothing about. We need to consider that. A 'yes' today is a yes for a long time. So I'd like it if you just thought it over for a day or two, and then we'll talk again. Is that okay?"

And so she agreed, and with wonder and excitement brightening her face, she went off to school, our future and Patrick's in her eleven-year-old but capable hands.

I should have known what to expect from Jane. She was not a selfish person. She was not given to jealousy or nitpicking. She was fair above all else. And she was an only child who did not particularly like that role.

It was Tuesday morning when I'd talked to her, and by Thursday evening at dinner, we planned a family discussion about the future, with or without Patrick. I'd tried to cook, but it hadn't turned out well, so I called Les and asked him to bring home pizza. It was a perfect choice. We were not distracted from the topic at hand by having to set the table or get a meal ready to eat.

The first thing I did was read Patrick's letter out loud. I wanted Jane to hear him introduce himself in his own words and learn a little more about him. A little more than his name, that is. Because it was a short letter, she was all ears. She had an air of anticipation, not worry or resentment or shame. It gave Les and me a feeling that everything was being thoughtfully considered with warmth and intelligence. But then again, maybe she was just an eleven-year-old girl excited for a change. I gave her credit, though. She was looking forward to the discussion.

Les had taken some notes and listed them in pros and cons. It was kind of sweet. There weren't many cons! So we went down the row of thoughts one at a time and came up with very little concern that things might not turn out well for all four of us. Yes, we agreed things would be thrown out of balance. Yes, we realized things might not turn out positively, and there could be disappointment. But as Jane said, all new things in life have these same wrenches in the works. And the good point was that Patrick obviously wanted to meet us, or at least me, and wasn't doing this letter-writing campaign to cause anyone trouble. At least, that's how it seemed.

We agreed our life together was filled with love and brightness. We felt we were wise enough to realize that this event

100

could end all of that if it turned sour. You can't really tell, you know, how you are going to react to change, even change you encourage. We spent an hour or more throwing ideas at each other, challenges we might face, and joys we might uncover. Ultimately, we decided we were strong allies and could withstand this very big hurdle. Jane got up from the table and fetched paper and a pen. I wrote Patrick a letter. We all contributed. It was a group effort.

"Dear Patrick," I wrote,

"There is a good chance that I am your mother. I am not sure of the steps you have taken to establish this, but I did give up a baby boy for adoption the month you were born in the same hospital where you were born. I have often thought of you over the years, wondering where you are, how you are, and what you are like. Mostly I've wondered if you are happy, and it sounds like you are! I'm so glad! I'm sure there are questions you would like to ask me, and I can only anticipate what they are. I think it would be best if they were answered in person and not on paper so that you can see how I feel when I talk, and I can judge your reactions better.

"Several years after your birth, I finished school and went to college, where I met my husband, Les. We have an eleven-year-old daughter named Jane. Les and Jane have been part of my decision-making. They both have agreed they would like to meet you. But more than that, we do not take family lightly and would like to know if you feel the same way. Since you have searched me out, I assume you have spent some time on this endeavor, which indicates you have more than a casual interest in meeting. We are, of course, curious, but also, at this point, and after some consideration, we are committed to trying to establish some kind of relationship with you.

"So, yes, I would love to have you come and visit us for coffee or more. Please let me know when that would be good for you. I am pretty open about times."

All three of us signed the letter to make it a more personal invitation. We sent along our phone numbers and a little indication of our weekly schedules. And at last, a picture of the three of us. I popped it in the mailbox Friday morning. And then we waited.

101

I lived for a few weeks on pins and needles, checking the mailbox every day just as it was closed by the mail person. After awhile, I got less worried about a response because I began to feel there wouldn't be one. Each day when Jane or Les got home, there were raised eyebrows and silent questions, but the mail didn't bring another letter, and we finally thought that maybe Patrick just didn't really want to meet us. Or me, at least.

I began to have doubts as to whether I wanted to meet him! I started to picture all the wrong that could be the outcome of our spending time together. I began to wonder if he were a legitimate son of mine or if he had lost interest. Or perhaps he was a scam artist of some sort. My imagination was roaming the countryside finding all sorts of awful scenarios.

And then one day, after about six weeks, there was a letter. It was not from Patrick. It was from his adoptive mother. She apologized for the delay in writing. She said Patrick had come to her to talk about his birth parents, that he had been doing an investigation and wanted to meet up with the woman he thought was his mother. She was hesitant but didn't want to spoil this for him. He'd been asking about his parents for years and was so curious. Besides that, he was no longer a boy. He was a man and settled enough in himself to handle this meeting.

The timing was bad, she said. Patrick had become sick just days after he'd sent the letter to me. It turned out to be COVID. He didn't fare well. He was in a coma for a couple of weeks before he could no longer breathe one afternoon.

When Marian and her husband Jim went home from the hospital after his death, they found our letter in the mail that had been collected in their box for 4 or 5 days. At first, they didn't know what it was or who I was, but after reading the letter, they remembered that Patrick had been working to find and meet his birth mother, and so they assumed that he had found her.

"It's taken me a few weeks to put together a few things that I wanted you to have. Writing this letter was the hardest part, and

102

therefore there was this delay. Your long-lost child has indeed been lost forever.

"Patrick was my only child. I want to thank you, Rita, for the opportunity to be a mother, the joy it brought me, and the fulfillment. Come and visit. I will take you to his grave.

"Patrick's funeral took place a few days after his death. It was there that I met and fell in love with a young lady, a friend of Patrick's, I assumed. It turned out that this 'friend' was Patrick's fiancé. He'd not told us about her yet but was planning to in a few weeks. Allison is a true delight.

"But I have saved the best for last: She is pregnant with Patrick's son! She told us she wants to share this child —both love and responsibility— with Patrick's family. That includes you now.

"Please come," she wrote. "Please come. The baby is due in 3 months." It would be my chance to bond with the baby I gave up so long ago—a new baby I would be encouraged to hold and love.

My heart broke for her more than for me. Patrick was her child for 24 years of ups and downs, and all that motherhood involves. I was so glad I could give her this son we shared. I was devastated that I would never meet him but would learn more about him when I met Marian and Jim a few weeks later. I would meet Allison. I would one day meet his son, my grandchild! There was a joy to be found in the future. So I planned my trip, our trip. We all would go and meet Patrick's family.

But not Patrick. I would never meet Patrick. He was a dream child I gave up at 15. He was not ever really mine.

The Travel Companion

Summer led Laura up the unstable aisle of the moving train. It was 1966, and the train was westbound for Seattle. Laura had boarded in Montana, heading for a business meeting. An attractive woman of 35, Laura had a classic look. With an Italian bag and leather briefcase, she wore a navy blue business suit, shoes to match her bag, Chanel No. 5, and a stylish bubble hairstyle.

Summer got on the train at a whistle stop near the Idaho – Washington border. She'd tumbled breathlessly into the seat facing Laura. A college student headed for UC Berkeley, she wore a knitted shawl, a long flowery skirt, and Birkenstocks. Her bag was a duffle with peace sign patches, her purse a macramé bag that hung from her shoulder. Her blonde hair curled and bounced, wild and free. She trailed an aura of cigarette smoke and Blue Grass cologne.

Laura's life was like the index of a book—everything was planned well in advance, organized, and listed in a perfectly rational order. But, when she traveled, Laura took a giant step outside her real life and met people and had experiences she would never have had if she had stayed home. Jostling along on the way to the dining car, Laura thought back to the afternoon she had just spent in the company of Summer.

How odd travel was! She found it amazing that she'd been having a marvelous time in the company of this sassy, unpredictable girl. Summer's fresh attitude left Laura feeling younger. Her off-the-wall stories about her classes, protests in the park, drugs, music, art, and her band of hippie friends had Laura laughing out loud and reconsidering her long-held opinions. Summer had a gift of gab. Listening to the astonishingly detailed stories of her escapades was like taking a plunge into a mountain spring-- shocking, delightful, and hilarious.

After lurching in single file through two train cars, Summer turned to Laura. "What a strange pair we must seem to the other passengers -- you with your fancy leather purse and me with my macramé bag!" she laughed. "I wonder what weird thoughts we inspire, what stories are being made up as we pass." Summer tossed her wayward hair and walked on, carelessly bumping seat after seat on her way up the aisle.

Watching her, Laura realized that she was trying with all her might to *avoid* contact of any kind with the seats along the way. Was her life really so controlled? She let go just a smidgen and bumped the back of the next seat with her hip. She felt an unfamiliar tug of pleasure. Maybe her life required a few bumps along the way.

As the two women entered the connecting compartment and opened the door to the dining car, the aroma of garlic and the tart smell of lemon wafted toward them. When the door closed behind them, the roaring of the moving train became indistinct, and the warm surroundings filled instead with the sounds of silverware connecting with dishes and the low voices of the crew. A linen tablecloth and a small lit lamp adorned each table. Draperies were drawn over the windows covering the darkness outside and giving the dining room an air of coziness. The activity was at a fever pitch for the crew, with everyone working together to get ready to serve dinner. A waiter was folding napkins in the butler's pantry near the door. He smiled and helped them find a seat. Since only two tables were occupied, this chivalry was unnecessary but expected by the class of people who frequented train dining cars. Summer whisked open the enormous menu and immediately spotted her heart's desire. Down went her menu just as Laura was lifting and opening her own.

Summer looked up at the waiter over her wire-rimmed glasses and told him she would have the prawns with drawn butter, rice, and a green salad. She looked at Laura expectantly. Laura sighed.

"Hmm, well," she said, "I'll have the same thing. And please, could you also bring me a glass of Chardonnay?" She had no idea why she ordered the prawns. She felt Summer was impatient for her to order, and she was so hungry that it didn't really matter. The wine was her way of being an individual, evidently.

The ice in their water glasses swayed in rhythm to the train, rocking like tiny boats at sea. They watched their waiter make his way to the kitchen. When he disappeared beyond the door, Summer hissed across the table at Laura,

"Do you have any money?"

"Why? Don't you?" Laura asked, her eyebrows raised. She felt like she'd just been shaken awake from a lovely dream.

"No. I was so broke I could barely get to the train station. Wait until they ask me for my ticket! That's going to be a scream."

Laura's face went white. Summer had just ordered a $12 dinner and had no money! In addition, she had no ticket. Had she assumed Laura would pay for her dinner? What in the world made her think that Laura had enough money to pay for a second dinner? And what gave her the idea that Laura would be willing to pay in the event she *did* have the money? Laura was downright angry. What exactly did Summer take her for? These damn hippies were so presumptuous. How could she have let her guard down?

In the meantime, Summer sat across the table, peeking between the drapes, humming a little tune, obviously not caring two shakes about the alarm she was causing in Laura's head. Though she did care that Summer was a thief, Laura was more upset that Summer would presume to use *her*. Had she been courted all afternoon as a meal ticket?

"Laura, you look like you're going to have a coronary!" Summer said. "What are you upset about anyway? If you're irritated with me, you don't need to be. I haven't done anything to you."

"Summer, you simply cannot get on a train without a ticket. You cannot order a $12 meal without the money to pay for it. How can you find this enjoyable? I would be worried sick that I would get caught! How can you be so uninvolved, so irresponsible?"

Summer leaned across the table, her back ramrod straight, chin up, her smile arrogant. Clutching a table knife in her fist, she said,

"This is ME, Laura. You sound like my parents! I may not be like them or like you, and that might be disappointing, but the truth is this is the way I am! I do whatever I want. I won't change to please you or anyone else because I'm *free*. The world lets people like me get by because most people are jealous of the life I live. They wish they had the guts to be more like me. I don't have to answer to anyone!"

"Of course, you're free, Summer!" Laura said. "But you're wrong if you think people find you amusing or are envious of you. More likely, they are disgusted by your behavior. You think people look the other way and allow you to be the way you are because they *admire* you. In reality, they look the other way to avoid the sight of you because they *don't give a damn* about you or what you do.

"But it's *because* you're free that you have the ability to change, and not just your life, but the world. You should start by respecting other people and their hard work and the hours they put in to make the things and provide the services you seem to think you can take without payment!"

"Oh, give me a break, Laura. I mean, Your Highness," Summer snapped. "I am showing you the way to freedom. If everyone were like me, the world would change and change for the better! Some corporation owns this train, and that corporation is the only thing I am hurting. Quit acting like a victim. I am an example of what life should be!"

"You are living in a dream world if you think that people will follow you, will listen to you, and find you enlightening. That they will think your protests and ideas for a new way of life are genuine. If that is what you believe, you are just plain mistaken! Summer, pay attention to me! NO ONE will listen to you if they don't respect you! Start by respecting yourself, girl!"

"Whoa!" was Summer's reply. "You are way out there, man. No way can I eat with someone as uptight as you." She stood up and, with a swirl of her skirt and a flick of her shawl, left the table. Laura sat with her mouth open for a minute before she signaled the waiter.

"My companion decided she wasn't hungry. I hope it's not too late to cancel her meal?"

"Not at all, Madame. Consider it done. If you would like company at your table, I'm sure others will come in to dine alone. Just let me know, and I'll seat someone with you." He turned back to the butler's pantry, water pitcher in hand.

Laura looked past him at Summer's retreating figure, her sloppy hairdo and string bag trailing behind her ridiculous swagger.

"Not on your life!" she muttered, "Not on your everlovin' life."

Your Butt

When you made the appointment, you said, "It's back pain." But it's deep in your left buttock in what feels like a joint, maybe where your thigh joins your back. It just hurts… and the longer it hurts, the less likely you are to be able to describe it.

On the appointed day, you go in. You are huddled against the pain. You are put in a room. The nurse enters and touches your back. She says, "Does it hurt here?"

"No," you say, "lower." "Show me," she says. You touch your butt where it hurts. "Oh," she says, "It hurts in your butt?" "Yes," you say, "in my left buttock." "Oh," she says and leaves.

The doctor comes in. "How are you?" he says. "I'm in pain," you say. He plays with his computer and other toys and then says, "Okay. Stand up and show me where it hurts."

"Here," you say.

"Oh," he says, "Your butt."

"Yes," you say, "My left buttock."

"Hm," he says, "Well. Not your back, really, then?"

"Well," you say, "Where my back ends, I guess."

"And how bad is the pain?" he asks.

"Eight," you say. "I am not bundled up sobbing, but it hurts damn bad."

"And how does it feel?" he asks.

111

"Hot, sharp, continual," you say.

"Not a dull ache?" he asks.

You get impatient with his lack of listening skills. "No!" you snap. He does not touch you. "It's a bone," you say.

"What?" he asks.

"A bone," you say, "It's hard as a bone. I think it's a bone."

"Hmm," he says. "Not a muscle?"

"No," you say.

He writes. "Take these pills for pain. Do these exercises. Use heat, then ice. Take it slow." He shoves a prescription at you and a pamphlet on exercises. "Call me in 2 weeks if it's not better." You turn white and start to sweat. *Two Weeks!* You think, panic near your heart. He zips out the door, not looking back. He does not touch you.

You fill your prescription, take hot baths, and do the stretches. The pain persists.

Ten days pass. You call. The doctor's out of town, but he can see you on the exact day he told you to call.

You hobble back in. The pain is no better. The nurse comes in and asks you again where the pain is, though she wrote it down last time. She sends the doctor in, and he asks you the same questions as last time. Finally, the doctor sends you to get an X-ray.

They show you a very flat table, higher up than your hip. They tell you to climb up on the table, and then they tell you, "Lay flat on your back." You try. It hurts so badly! You cry out. The tech doesn't touch you. She stands back and waits. "Flat?" you ask. "Yes," she says, "Just for a moment." You squirm and settle. "Hurry!" you whisper.

She leaves the room and sends cancer-causing rays out at you. When she returns, she helps you to sit up. It's a good thing. If she hadn't, you would be lying there still. It hurts even with her help. Nothing will ever feel good again.

In three days, they call to say, "The X-ray shows nothing. Going now for an MRI." "Okay," you say, "When?" "Next Tuesday," they say. "Nothing sooner?" you ask. "No, sorry," they say. You don't believe they are sorry.

You manage. But you don't know how you do it. Your memory of these three weeks will only be of pain, pills, heat, and ice.

You go in for the MRI. "Where does it hurt?" asks the receptionist. "Here," you say. "Oh," she says and writes on a chart. The technician comes out for you and says to put on a hospital gown. You have spent an hour putting on your clothes. You are not sure you can get them off now! You manage. You leave your socks on.

The technician meets you in the hall with a clipboard. "Where does it hurt?" she asks. You touch your backside. Your lips are clenched, and you can't speak. "Oh," she says, "Your butt?" "Yes," you manage to croak. "My left buttock. Deep." She hurls you up on a cold table and props your limbs with pillows and cushions. She does not touch your painful butt.

You are warm and fall asleep to the banging of the MRI machine. You are awakened by silence and are distressed that you have to leave. It was so warm!

When the pictures are completed, your doctor calls you in. He doesn't actually call you. He has someone call you. When you arrive two days later at his convenience, he shows you the test results. He touches them. He touches the butt on the page as he would not touch yours.

"You can see here that you have an old hamstring injury," he says. You are dumbfounded. "Hamstring?" you say, "in my butt?" "Yes," he says. He leaves you alone with your mouth hanging

113

open. A nurse comes in and gives you a referral for physical therapy. You make it home and call to set up the appointment. "Where is your pain?" they ask you. "In my left buttock," you say. "In your butt, then?" they ask. "Yes," you say, "in my butt." "Come in on Monday at 10," they say.

The pain goes on. Monday continues to stay days and days away. At last, 10:00 AM Monday arrives. You go to the physical therapist's office. In the room, he asks you, "When did you first injure your hamstring?" "I don't know," you say, "my butt just started hurting one day last month." "Your butt?" he asks. "Yes," you say. "Can you show me where it hurts then?" he asks. "Yes," you say, and point to your left buttock. "Here," you say, "In my butt."

"Hmmm," he says. "Well, let's put heat on it first." He leaves the room. The assistant comes in. "I'll put some heat on your injury," she says. "Show me where it hurts." "Here," you say, pointing to your left buttock. "In your butt?" she asks. "Yes," you say. "In my butt." She puts something warm and moist on your backside. It feels good from your toes to your hairline. You moan. *Never take it off!* You plead, in your head.

She takes the heat off in exactly 7 minutes. You miss it instantly. You wish you had the strength to take it back from her and put it on your butt again. But the warmth has dissolved you into pudding. The assistant helps you up and then drags you out to a mat, where she thrusts you down and makes you do exercises. Bend knees, pull legs up, twist, etc. Over and over. You just want the heat back.

"Get on this machine now," she says. She peels you off the floor and applies you to the machine in question, where you are required to walk if you don't want to be rolled out onto the floor. You walk and walk, fast then slow, for a very long time. You feel you may have walked to San Francisco. The assistant turns the machine off, and you stop walking.

"Take Tylenol," she says. "Do your exercises and come back in 3 days." "Will I get the heat again?" you ask. "Yes," she says,

114

"And some time on the machine!" "Just the heat," you say. "I only want the heat!" She laughs. "I know it feels good," she says, "but the exercises will help you feel better soon."

You go home. You take your Tylenol and do your stretches. When you return on Thursday, you are surprised that you can get up on the table without help. The heat still feels good, but not as much like Heaven as you thought on Monday. You walk on the machine. It's better.

Each time you go, it gets better. It keeps getting better and better.

Finally, the physical therapist tells you not to come back. You are cured. You can sit anywhere without pain; you can climb hills and run after a bus.

You go home. Happy. Your butt doesn't hurt anymore. In a week, you stop remembering how happy you were that day. You just keep walking. You sit anywhere. You walk the dog. You feel wonderful, and you take your butt and health for granted.

Saint's Day

When Megan opened her eyes, the sky was a mass of spangles—a million colors, bright and shiny. She got up from the cement park bench where she'd slept the night before. Dragging her rucksack off the ground, she hoisted it onto her shoulder.

Megan's hair stuck out in all directions, wild and crazy, with curls in five shades of blond. Her teeth felt nasty. She dug in her pocket for the box of mints she'd picked up off the sidewalk the day before and popped one in her mouth. She bit into it. Mint, and lots of it, flew up behind her eyes and made them pop. Her nose started to tickle. She sneezed—a whopper. A squirrel, running across the path, jumped at the sound.

Megan hollered at him, "Run, you little bastard!" She burst into laughter and laughed until her sides hurt, and her eyes ran with tears. The squirrel did not come back. He ran from Megan just as everyone did.

Megan had walked only 20 feet when she abruptly dropped her sack and sat down on the sidewalk to look at the color collection in the sky. It was so awesome. The naked tree limbs were dancing and shaking themselves to some inner music. Megan was sure she could hear it. It sounded like the 1812 Overture, but maybe she was on the wrong channel.

A man appeared and stared at her as he circled. "Hey, Toots!" he yelled, whistling like a train. His overcoat was long, way too long. It nearly touched the ground around his feet. He had the best and most colorful scarf and wore a tipped Fedora on his head. Megan was pretty sure she knew him, but she could not remember his name or where she knew him from. It might be a bad memory. He was small and quick. She studied the wrinkles in his face, brown and grey beard, and mustache. Her eyebrows arched up and over her nose, and a deep wrinkle took form as she tried hard to remember. She pulled a purple stocking cap out of her bag and down onto her head. She glared at the man.

He continued to circle her, smiling and muttering. Megan wasn't sure about him. Was he a friend, she wondered? He squatted. Stared into her face.

"Toots! Don't avoid me, Toots! Look here, look here! It's me, Miraculous Joe! You know me, Toots. I'm your friend! We go way back, you and me." Still, Megan was unsure.

"Get back, you!" she yelled. She stuck out her arms, palms open, like she was stopping traffic. "Get back, you hear!" She would not rise and run, afraid he would follow. "What do you want anyway?"

"Come on, Toots! I've been away awhile, but I'm back now. Let's go to the shelter and get us something to eat just like we used to," Joe said. He wasn't being silly anymore. She started to think the memory might be a nice one. He put out his hand. She hesitated before she reached for it. Megan was not one for touching. Joe helped her up. His hand was warm. She picked up her bag and followed him out of the park and down the early morning street, where tiny green leaves sprouted on the trees.

"Joe, I'm not sure I remember you. Why don't I know you if you know me?" she said to his back as they walked.

"Maybe it's this beard," he said, half turning. "When I went to my sister's, I didn't have it. I didn't hurry back either. I stayed a long time. You and I used to go to the shelter for dinner together almost every day. Do you remember that? Maybe you remember that." He cocked his head and looked at her.

"Joe, look at the sequin sky!" Megan urged him in a loud voice. "Look at all the colors and designs!"

Joe stopped and looked where Megan pointed. He didn't seem to see sequins. For all she could tell, he saw only grey rain clouds, plump and full. His face looked like a question mark. Maybe to him, the sky was all the exact same color. It wasn't. To Megan, it was all the colors of the world.

"Come on now, Toots," he said, turning back to her. "Can't you just smell that bacon cookin'? They have pancakes, and they have bacon, and hot coffee. You come with old Joe, and you won't be sorry."

"I don't eat much," Megan said. She followed Joe anyway. He was a good leader. She seemed to remember that much.

* * *

The shelter was warm and smelled good. The weather had been nice for a few weeks, and beds were sometimes empty. Joe led Megan to the line for chow. She dragged her bag along at her side. She wasn't sure where her things went, but she constantly came up short a thing or two. She couldn't trust anyone. Barely anyone.

A lady in a pretty red dress stood behind a serving counter. Steam rose from the chrome serving tray in front of her. It twisted in and around her shiny white hair, trimmed and curled. She handed Megan a plate full of scrambled eggs and bacon and told her to get a cup of coffee at the end of the line. When she spoke, she had the voice of an angel. Megan didn't want to move along. It smelled good near the hot food containers, and the lady was smiling. She looked at Megan and said,

"Did you see that sunrise this morning? The sky was every shade of color! It was almost startling, don't you think? I had to pull my car over to take a better look!" Megan turned and hurried off to catch up with Joe at the coffee line. She wondered why he hadn't seen the same sparkling sky as she and this red-dressed lady. She poked him. He did not look at her.

"Miraculous," she said, "Did you hear what that lady said? She saw the sequins in the sky, the same as me. I wonder why you didn't see them. Joe?" She touched his sleeve again.

119

Joe whirled on her. He was glaring, and his look frightened her. She saw that his eyes were blazing and his hair was on fire. She wasn't sure when it had caught the flame. She backed away and took her food to a table.

"Damn that, Joe. I wanted coffee. Why would he act so mean for no reason?" The lady next to Megan looked at her curiously. "Are you okay?" she said. She was skinny and dressed in bright green from top to bottom. Her teeth were awful, brown, and bent, with some missing. Her hair stuck out from underneath a baseball cap with the bill turned to the side. The angle of the green hat made her look wrong, like a boy.

Megan picked up her plate and moved to a table by the wall. She placed her sack in front of the bench and put her feet on it when she sat down. She curled her arm around her food and ate, looking up over the top of her elbow at the people in the room. She bent low and scooped up her eggs with her fingers. She'd forgotten to pick up a fork.

Abruptly a lot of yelling came from the other side of the room. Megan turned to see what was going on. Fearing that someone was coming after her, she reached down and clutched the strap of her bag just in case she had to run.

Miraculous Joe was pushing someone. His hair was still aflame. He held bolts of lightning in his hands. Megan barely recognized him from when he'd squatted to stare at her in the park. He looked determined now. His skin was tight and white, and his eyes had turned icy blazing blue. Megan pushed her back up to the wall and tried to disappear.

She heard more hollering and some furniture smashed to the floor. A man followed, tumbling down, his shoe flying into the air. As it fell, it whacked a little boy on the head. The boy cried out. The boy's father jumped up and started to swing left and right.

Megan grabbed her sack and ran for the door. People were shuffling forward around the fighting men. Megan shoved her way through the crowd. Body odors assailed her nostrils, awful odors of smoke, coffee, tar, grease, popcorn, syrup, candy, sweat, and bad breath all mixed together. Too many people! It was hot and too crowded, and Megan began to breathe hard.

When she broke through the mass of bodies, she flew to the door and rammed it with her bent arms. She gasped as the fresh air hit her smack in the face. It was wonderful! She threw her arms straight out and turned in circles on the sidewalk. Round and round, she went, looking straight up at the sky. The clouds she saw above her mixed and mingled and became, at last, a long strand of white that circled her like a halo. She felt holy, and it was no wonder. The halo made her a saint.

* * *

Megan sat on another bench in the park. Hardwood seats were better than concrete because they were warmer, but still, they were awfully hard on her bottom. When she closed her eyes and nibbled on the piece of pizza she'd found in the park trash, she could pretend she was in a nice warm house with cushioned chairs. She made up a story about her birthday and how she'd asked for pizza and her wish had been granted. She was maybe 40 again, or she might be just 35. Lots of people came to celebrate with her in the fancy house. They brought her presents and stood by, admiring her saintliness. Everything was clean.

She just now realized that instead of a pretend birthday, today was her Saint's Day! When she opened her eyes, she looked at the world differently. She knew she could levitate if she wanted to, but she chose to walk instead. She got up slowly, picked up her bag, and headed for the cathedral on Fifth Avenue. In this church, she knew she would find out her True Name. Megan was surely not her saint's name -- it was just too simple for a saint.

"I'm coming, Lord!" She called out. "Be thinkin' up my new name. I'll be there pretty soon!" Two boys walking near her stopped to stare. She turned to them and squealed, "OOOOw, nasty little boys, I'm a saint, and you better watch out." When they continued to gape at her, she boomed, "I have the ear of God!" The boys turned and ran. Megan heard them gasping. She was sure they were crying with fear. She imagined their tears filling bucket after bucket, all falling over, starting a river that flowed to the sea. "May the river wash away your sins!" she called after them.

A cat meowed from a window three stories up. Megan looked up the side of the red brick building and smiled at the cat. "Don't be afraid, Kitty," she called. "No one can hurt you up there in the window!" She smiled at the cat and tossed the rest of her pizza slice up the wall in his direction. The cat snarled and jumped back into the room behind him.

Megan saw him disappear. She was amazed and awed by his abilities.

At the corner, just beyond the cat's home, Megan once again ran into Joe, leaning back against the side of a building. He had crumbs in his thick beard. His hat was tipped onto the back of his head so that she could see his eyes had calmed to a shimmery blue, like the sky, like a lake. She approached him, tapping out a little tune with her footsteps. He didn't seem to see her coming.

"Joe!" she called. She walked up to him and looked right in his face. She remembered now that Joe couldn't see well. "I'm on my way to church. I'm going to get my saint's name from God!" Joe looked back at Megan, a smile turning up the corners of his mouth. He winked at her.

"Can I go with you?" he asked. "I can always use a meeting with God."

"God will be happy to see us both. I know it!" she said. "He tells me things."

Joe put his hand on Megan's shoulder for support and slowly moved away from the wall. Megan heard him sigh, and his knees cracked. "Would you like me to carry your bag for you," he said. "It looks heavy."

She moved the bag to her other side. Her bag was the one load she didn't want to share. She considered his offer. She considered him. She handed him the bag.

"Let's skip!" she said. She grabbed his hand and began a rolling, jumping gait that vaguely resembled skipping but was really more like hopping. She watched the sidewalk, fearful of stepping on a crack and breaking her mother's back or tripping over some cement raised or cracked by a root. She had to really hold on to Joe. He wasn't much of a skipper. "Tell me how you get that fire in your hair," Megan said.

"I don't know what you mean," Joe said. He turned away, and when he looked back, his face had changed. His mouth turned down at the corners, and his eyes looked like broken glass. "I don't know what you mean by that," he said again.

"When we were at the shelter," Megan said. "Remember, Joe? Remember when we were at the shelter for breakfast, and the red-dress lady said the sky was so full of color, and then your eyes turned to ice, your hair turned to fire, and you had lightning in your hands? Remember when that shoe hit the boy in the head, flying out of space and whacking him so hard? And all those people came pushing forward? Do you remember, Joe?"

Joe raised his eyebrows. He slowed and dropped her hand. He slowed even more until, finally, they'd stopped skipping and stood still on the sidewalk, looking at each other. "A lady fell," Joe said. "A man behind her in the coffee line started to kick her. I told him to stop, but he didn't stop. He didn't listen. I hit him. I don't remember the lightning or anything else. But that man, he was so cruel. It made me very sad and so angry."

"Your hair had flames in it, and your eyes were lit up like sparklers," Megan told him. "A lot of people stood up to watch you. Too many people. I had to leave then because the room started to crumple up like a ball of tinfoil."

Joe said, "I didn't know that happened. I was only trying to help the lady who fell. I was only trying to help." His voice faded away. His face drooped. For the first time, Megan thought Joe looked old and tired.

"Well," said Megan, "We'll just go to the big church, and I'll get my saint's name. It's just here around this corner. Don't worry, Joe. God likes you, fine. You'll be welcome in his house. I can promise you that."

When they rounded the corner, Joe stood back. His hands had returned to his pockets, and he looked down at the sidewalk. Megan pulled one of his hands out of a pocket. Holding his hand through her bent arm, she led him along up the steps and in through the enormous carved door that boomed shut behind them when Megan let it drop from her grasp. They stood in the dark vestibule, both taking in the sights before their eyes. There was so much gold – gold frames and gold arches and golden lanterns. There was so much paper, too--piles of paper and many books. There was so much writing stacked around. Words and words and words! Megan wondered what could be so important.

"Can you read what's on these pages, Joe?" she asked.

"Toots, I can't seem to read," he said. He stroked his beard. His face looked soft. "I try, but it's an art that I don't have. Why? Can't you?"

Megan took a deep breath. "I can't seem to do it either," she said. "Someone tried to show me once a long time ago. I was a terrible learner." She turned away, looked at all the important papers, and sighed. Quietly she moved toward another set of double doors with square brass handles. "Come on, Joe," she hissed. "We go in here. This is where the saints live, and God gives out their names. We might have to wait in line." She pulled Joe into the church through one of the doors. It whooshed shut and settled with a loud thud as it closed.

Joe said, "I think I'll just sit here for awhile, Toots. I'm feelin' a little poorly." He moved into the last pew and settled down, removing his hat and putting it on the bench beside him. He took a deep breath and then coughed. He pulled a little bottle from his pocket and drank something. Megan thought it was probably medicine. Soon his coughing stopped, and his head dropped back. He looked up to the ceiling. Megan, too, looked up. The ceiling was way far off. It was like the sky hanging above them, curved and round and holding them safely together. There were saints up there and maybe God, all floating above them and busy doing churchy things. When Megan picked up her bag, she looked back at Joe. His head had hit the back of the bench, and his eyes were closed. Without the fire of his eyes, he looked peaceful. Megan worried a bit about leaving him, but then she turned to the altar and began her long walk to God. "I'll just go look around and see if I can find out what we have to do," Megan whispered to herself, drifting slowly up the aisle.

The floor was smooth and shiny. On its white surface were lines and splashes of dark grey, sprouting from nowhere and dashing left and right. Megan's old shoes made an enormous racket as she walked toward the front of the church. "If you didn't know I was coming, you sure must know I'm here now!" she called out to God. Her voice sounded large and round and booming.

There were bright shards of colored light streaming and dancing all around Megan. She thought it was God saying HELLO and HOW NICE TO SEE YOU! But she wasn't sure. The light was pretty, but she didn't want to let it distract her. She was on a mission and needed to get on with it. When she got to the front of the church, she looked left and right, but she couldn't see God. She thought He should be there to meet her and anyone else who might come by, but there was just a big table with candles in gold stands and flowers in vases, a huge book, and a few other things set all about on top. She walked up the steps and saw that someone didn't seem to have the right tablecloth – it didn't go all the way to the edge of the narrow table, but just down the center. Then, in the end, it was too long and fell almost to the floor.

"I could have done this better," she muttered. There was a draft, and Megan looked up, thinking God had finally made an appearance. No one was there, but the candle flames blew sideways as if a wind were passing through. Behind the big table, she noticed a picture of a man that looked a little like Joe. He was in a long coat

125

and had a beard like Joe's though it was all brown with no grey. His eyes were lit up like Joe's were sometimes, too. He looked a little tired like he had more to do than energy to spare. She looked at him for a long time and felt good, like when someone smiled at her.

Without warning, a lady came up to Megan and touched her sleeve. "You must be Sally," she said. "Are you here to clean the church?" She pressed a broom into Megan's hands. "You can put your bag over on that bench if you want. It's safe there," she said.

Megan looked at the lady. She was plain and sweet. Her hair was soft and curled, and she smelled so clean. Her hands were worn and marked with use. But her eyes, well, her eyes were brilliant! Her eyes were like chunks of cracked emeralds, bright and glowing and lit from within. Megan took the broom and went to put down her bag. She began to sweep. She swept the church for hours and sang while she swept. She sang songs she hadn't heard in a very long time. Sometimes she forgot the words, and so she just made some up. The echo of her voice in the big church sounded wonderful, like in the movies!

Time had no meaning for Megan, but even so, it continued to slip by. When she reached the back of the church, she leaned over Joe and whispered, "Joe, I've met God. She's lovely! She told me my name—it's Saint Sally! I'm St. Sally! And today is my saint's day. And a very special day it is!" Joe opened his eyes and smiled at her. His lids were heavy, and he soon closed them and drifted off again.

St. Sally kept up the broom work, looking in wonder at the pictures around the church, the colored windows cut from tiny little pieces of glass, the statues that stood about in their long colorful robes with trays of candles at their feet, the odors of incense and furniture polish, the sparkle of the old wood, and the glow that seemed to come from nowhere to light up everything. When she finished, she went up the altar steps and tried to find God to return the broom. No one was there. She tilted the broom against the wall by the bench and left it there. She lifted her bag and slung it over her shoulder.

126

When she turned back to the church, the fancy lights dangling from the ceiling had come on. The windows were dark, and shadows crisscrossed, falling in every direction. It felt like she was in a forest with sunlight slipping through the trees in long lines. She walked slowly down the aisle, stepping in and out of the puddles of light, nearly afloat. She thought it was the quietest place she had ever been. As she neared the door, she saw that Joe was not where she'd left him.

Nearing the last pew, she felt another cool draft on her neck. Her hair lifted, a strand curling around and tickling her nose. She looked around for God to appear as she'd done earlier but saw no one. When she looked back at the bench, she saw Joe's hat just where it had been before, and there, too, was Joe, fallen over and still. He was sleeping very hard. "Come on, Joe, let's go," she said. "God's house is clean, and I have my new name. We can go now." Joe did not answer her. He did not open his eyes or smile. He did not move.

"Joe?" she said. "Joe, it's me, St. Sally! We can go now, Joe!" Still he didn't move. She touched his hand. His arm slipped over the side of the pew, and his fingers touched the floor. St. Sally picked up Joe's hand. She put it gently on his chest. She took off his shoes and set them on the floor. From her bag, she pulled a warm blanket from a thrift shop and tenderly tucked it around Joe, covering him from chin to toe, lifting his beard, and placing it carefully on top.

She stepped past Joe. She took a little towel out of her bag and, with some water from a bowl by the door, she wet her rag. She gently wiped his face clean and then his hands. She washed him and sang to him a lullaby she remember hearing somewhere. Then she sat near him on the pew and lifted his head into her lap. She brought out her comb and tugged softly at his beard to get the tangles out and finally she combed his hair. When she was done fixing Joe up, she settled back and looked up to the altar.

"God," she said, "It's me, St. Sally. Here's this nice man, Joe. I'm leaving him to you. He was kind to me and cared for me when no one else ever did. He made sure I ate and walked with me

127

so no one bad would bother me. He listened to me. It may seem like nothing to some, but it was so much to me! When his sleep is over, and he's done here with upsetting things, I hope that you will take him to heaven and be sure he can see colors there, and I hope that all the saints are good to him. Amen."

St. Sally stayed seated for an hour, just patting Joe's hands, stroking his beard, and watching his chest rise and fall. When she got up, she sighed and set his hat on the pew near him. She left her blanket to keep him warm. She bent then and kissed him on the forehead.

"Goodbye, Joe," she said. "Thank you for a very nice time." She went out the door then and out the other door. She carried her bag down the rugged stone steps, off down the street, and to the park, where she took her place on her familiar cement bench and silently watched the stars that sparkled like diamonds in the sky just for her.

Transition

The traffic isn't bad tonight. Though it's still spring, I feel Summer in the air. I turn up the radio and roll down the window of my five-year-old VW Bug. The warm coastal breeze blows through my hair. This is my first time alone all day, and I am determined to enjoy it!

This will be my last evening to drive this familiar route--my last night as a telephone operator, a job I've had for six years since I was 18. As of Monday morning, I will begin my new job. My transfer has come through at last! I will be an equipment maintainer for my company, a job previously not open to women. So tonight, I am wondering if I am doing the right thing. Taking a "man's job" will not gain me any points with my new co-workers—MEN. My life has been simple as an operator. I genuinely hope I am not causing more turbulence than I can handle.

As I near the square, gray, windowless building that has become like a second home to me, I begin to relax again. This is familiar; this is secure. I have made many memories here at the "Toll Office." Later tonight, I will clean out my locker, turn in my headset, and close the file on this phase of my life. Suddenly I find I am anxious to get on with things. The transition from my position as a new hire at my first job to where I am today—a wife, mother, homeowner, and an adult— is about over! I am ready for new challenges, another transition.

As I drive into the parking lot, my friend Nancy drives in behind me. I climb out of my car and notice the sun setting across Pacific Coast Highway. It's beautiful -- one of the best this year. Maybe smoke from the fire in Palos Verdes makes it so gorgeous, or maybe it's just for me. Nancy hollers, "Hi!" through a mouthful of peanuts (probably her dinner), and our car doors thump in unison.

We lock up our cars, head towards the door, with enough time to have a quick cup of coffee before we go on the board at six PM.

I'm glad Nancy is working with me tonight. We've been through so much together -- friends for all of my six years here. Working my last night here without her sitting beside me wouldn't seem right. She and I started at the phone company within a month of one another. It was the first job for both of us, and we became friends simply because we were thrown together. We shared similar unpopular shifts, breaks, and lunches. We found we liked so many of the same things: the same music, the flea markets, reading novels, cooking, and eventually, our kids. And we grew very close. Each of us was pleased to have a friend. She is the best thing I got from this job.

As I reach for the phone by the door to dial the code to release the lock, I am reminded of my first day. Fresh from high school and newly on my own, I had reached a trembling hand for the phone to ask someone to let me in. Once inside, I became one of the secret bearers: the secret of the door code, the secret of customer communications, the magic secret of telephone credit cards, and the secret behind every telephone--the Real People who are the Operators. These voices, heard by thousands, have become my sisters.

Inside now, the security door slams shut with a resounding boom. We climb the steep cement stairs, go to our meager grey lockers to deposit jackets, check the schedule to be sure we have the same breaks, and then go to the lunchroom for coffee. Plopping down at a round white Formica table, we light cigarettes, hoist our feet on empty chairs, and prepare to enjoy our first adult company all day. We both sigh.

"Did they buy me a cake?" I ask. I hate surprises, and Nancy always warns me.

"You know they did. Of course, they did!! I think they got it from Ruby's husband's bakery." We both laugh over this. Ruby's husband's bakery makes the worst cakes in town. We always swore whoever left first would have to eat a whole one herself.

"Did you see the smoke on the way to work?" I ask. "I heard on the news there's been a fire up in Palos Verdes since about 2:00." I'll be surprised if Nancy knows anything about this--she rarely listens to the news or reads a paper.

"Yeah, my mom called and said she had heard about it on the news. Something about an evacuation. For crying out loud! She knows about it clear out in Ohio!!" Nancy says.

We both know that this means it will be busy tonight. As in all emergencies, people pick up the phone. The supervisor appears at the break room door as if called up by my thoughts.

"Girls, it's a madhouse in there with the fire. Could you come in a few minutes early, please?" She looks frantically around the room, perhaps disappointed that only two of us are there. We assure her we will be right in, and she's gone. Nancy mutters something about being called a "girl" and dumps her coffee down the drain. We put out our cigarettes and gather up our things.

I remind myself that it's my last day at this job, in this office, and I try to figure out why I should be rushing to work. After all, why should I still care? But, I find I care as I always have cared. Someone may really need help. Houses are burning--no, homes are burning. People are desperate and afraid and need to hear a human voice. I care because once, an operator helped me when I was alone and told me to call back if everything wasn't okay. I'll never forget it. I try to pay that back on good nights with just a little more than service.

Nancy and I shuffle through the swinging doors, punch the time clock and put on our headsets.

"Try to sit by me," Nancy whispers. We locate two vacant positions and climb up on the stools. The longboard stretches out to my left and right. Operators perch on high metal stools wearing big ugly black headsets that flatten and destroy their ears. In front of us, panels of jacks and lights line up down the distance, their appearance repeating over and over down the board. On the desktop in front of us are the cord pairs, the back one for the customer's incoming call,

131

and the one closest to us we will plug in to complete their request. Our board is so old we still have dials. Touchpads are evidently a thing of the future here at the beach.

"I know one thing I won't miss when I leave," I tell my friend. "These stupid chairs!" Nancy laughs. She knows my shortness makes these stools uncomfortable. It has become one of my constant complaints.

It's very busy. Lights are standing on every panel. The supervisor is pacing. The clatter is unreal.

"Hi, Turkeys," says our friend Becky who works until midnight.

"Hi, Beck," we both say.

I plug in my headset and grab a ticket, a pencil, and a cord. Do a quick survey of supplies at my position. It's all so routine. Nancy asks if I have any extra scratch paper. I hand her some as I plug into my first call.

"Operator." Everything else disappears. The call is everything now.

Over the next few hours, each thing seems so significant. The last time, the last time, I keep thinking. I almost feel I will miss the customers. Coming in a few minutes early allows me to take six calls before my shift starts. One says, "God bless you," 2 are rude, and three are indifferent. Two busy circuits, one recording, and three calls were completed. They think I am not real. It plagues me. Sometimes they get so angry trying to prove I am not an actual person that I cry to prove that I am. Most of our customers assume that we are stupid. It's impossible to prove that they're wrong. I have almost learned to live with it.

Just at six o'clock, three of my friends come over to say goodbye, good luck, we'll miss you. These three have been part of my journey into the tunnel that is this job. They are wary of me now—I have seen the light at the end of the tunnel. I will break away. These three friends are unsure of how to talk to me.

Opening a key, I notify a coin customer before turning to them. "Three minutes; signal when through, please!" I close the key.

"Come and see us when you get adjusted," says Joan, who will never adjust to anything.

"You're so lucky! Almost ten bucks an hour and away from all this," says Chris, who has only been here a year and doesn't understand that luck has nothing to do with it. My transfer took two years to come through. It's the late1960s, and an operator is paid $2.00 an hour. What kind of life will this give these women, two of whom are raising kids alone?

"I'll call you when Jack and I have our next party," says Penny, who has the most outrageous parties ever. She knows I will never go. My coin customer is flashing. Opening the key, I tell him, "One moment, please."

Turning to my friends, I whisper, "Bye, you guys. Take care." Quick hugs all around. They all look like they're in pain. This is no place to say goodbye, especially while an emergency rages just over the hill, its smoke visible through the few windows on the south wall.

I know these friends won't be very happy about seeing me a month from now. I will no longer be in their special world. They will seem almost indifferent if I come in on my day off. I will be an outsider who only reminds them of the trap they are in. They won't want to hear more than a quick "Hey!"

And after all my homey thoughts about this familiar place where I spend a better part of each day, I will be sad a month from now to find out exactly how easily my friendship has been replaced. Like a slap in the face, I'll realize why an office (my first office) is only an office, and really not a family.

When we were new here, each of us took one look at some of the older operators and said to ourselves, "I sure won't be around when I'm THAT old. This is just a starting place for ME." But it becomes much easier to stay after awhile than to move on. When someone comes back to visit with stars in their eyes, we all move out of the beam. We act indifferent. Our time hasn't come. We are not yet ready for a change. Some never are.

We stick together and try to make the most of our days. We have parties. We take care of each other. And we get by. One by one, we leave for whatever reason. And those left behind re-evaluate their choices with each parting.

I reach over and pat Nancy on the arm. "HUH?" she says. I shake my head and smile. I'm missing her already. A lone woman in my new office, with much to learn and many adjustments, I will, at times, be overcome with loneliness. She will still be here among our friends. Secure, at least, though maybe dissatisfied.

"Your overtime is 20 cents, sir." Bing bing bing bing. "Thank you." Clunk.

Sigh. "I'll be so glad to be away from this," I think for the thousandth time. But talk to me six years from now. Maybe by then, I'll realize it's not a rut or a prison. It's a job, and that's life. I have made many a memory and many a friend here. It has been a happy/sad time—only a starting place for some, a lifetime for others.

And so the night goes on. Friends saying goodbye, a last report from my supervisor who came in just for this, a cake to cut at lunch break, and I feel like I'm gone already. By 10:30, when business begins to die down, I almost feel like I'm a spectator. I have been feeling on the outside all night long. Watching. Recording. I begin to realize my regrets about leaving; my attachment to this life. I grow quiet. I am afraid of leaving.

Nancy and I take our last break together at 11:45. She's mad at me for leaving. She doesn't say it, but the look is there. It's quiet in the lunchroom after the office noise, the clicking, buzzing, and

134

hushed voices. We get our coffee, put our feet up, and light cigarettes.

"I'm sorry," I say.

"It's Okay, really," she pretends, actually on the verge of tears. "I understand that you have to do something new. I encouraged you, for God's sake! I get that the money is great compared with this and that the kids cost more every day. But somehow, understanding doesn't make it any easier. I love coming to work when you're scheduled, too. You know...I'm just going to miss you."

"I'm really so sorry," I say again. I just don't know what more I can say. "You know I'll miss you, too. And we WILL see each other, though I know it won't ever be the same."

Then she gives me a present! It is unexpected and exciting. She has had it in her yarn bag all night. All she says is, "Here." There is no card. So I open it without comment. I open it slowly to make it last, savoring the moment.

It's a photo album. All the pictures she's promised me copies of for six long years: together at the beach--skinny, tan, and single; together with our new husbands going to another friend's wedding; together pregnant--round and sunny; together at our baby shower; together with babies, at the park; at birthday party number 1, on through my next pregnancy, our children hugging the new baby, our children with pudding on their faces, our children on matching potty chairs.

The pictures inspire me and touch me. Our friendship is one of the best things that has ever happened to me. The second to the last page is a poem she's written for me. The end reads,

"But this, my friend,

Is how I remember you best."

I turn the page and find a picture of me in a headset, sitting at the board. Nothing special--just my hair a tangle on any busy day, pencil and cord in hand, leaning slightly forward as if that would help me to hear or understand a customer better. I never even knew she had taken this picture.

My camera freak, my poet, my friend. How will I ever replace you? Always thoughtful, always available, always strong.

"You're unbelievable," I sniffle. "You make me believe I may miss this wretched place."

"Come on. It's time to go back," she says.

Arms around each other, together we head towards the swinging doors for the last time.

The War of the Chicken

The war began just two weeks ago. You would not have read about it in the papers or seen it on the evening news. This was intimate, horrific, a domestic squabble of sorts.

On Tuesday, I stalked the aisles of the Stop and Shop, a sinister hunter looking for a defenseless chicken. I did not hesitate when I spotted the sign — "Tender Young Chicken." I snatched him by his package and thrust him into my cart with disdain. I had no idea the battle he would wage. Tender Young Chicken, indeed.

Upon returning home, I carried the headless wonder to the garage. He was no match for me. I yanked open the freezer door and pushed him in. I was not prepared for his rebellion. He rolled toward the door and jammed himself in the opening so I could not close it. I heard him sliding and struggling on the other side. I kept pushing. Finally, I reopened the door and wedged him near the back, quickly slamming the door to keep him within.

On Thursday, I went to the freezer for pork chops. I crept slowly and quietly so as not to alert the chicken, but he must have read my mind. He was waiting for me! Once again, I heard him squirming. It sent shivers up my spine. As I yanked the door ajar, the chicken jumped out and fell on my foot with a thud. I had to re-evaluate the situation. I could not let this rock-hard fowl get the best of me! With both hands extended, I bent to seize him. Just as I lunged and got a good grip on his frozen thighs, the door swung shut and bashed me in the head.

But the chicken was mine. I did not release him. This time I moved everything off the shelf on the door of my opponent's bastillion, the icy dark freezer. I jammed him in good and

137

surrounded him with packages of frozen vegetables. There I left him to cluck his silent best until today. He'd had more than a week to prepare. I wasn't sure how safe I would be disturbing him.

This morning at six AM, I once again approached the freezer. I heard a struggle, but it was much diminished. When I made contact with the door, the struggle ceased. Opening the door swiftly, I interrupted his attempts to hurl himself to freedom by grabbing him in both hands with a towel.

I carried the poultry to the kitchen sink at arm's length. There I floated him in water, which acted like a moat—not to block invaders but to keep my nemesis inside.

When I came home at 3 PM, I took scissors and cut away the plastic sack with its deceiving label. The wretched chicken remained frozen on the inside. I slid my hand into his neck orifice to drag out his essential organs, but my hand became stuck. I whacked him on the counter as my hand became colder and colder. He would not release me! Desperate, I clutched his heart and ran hot water inside his cavity. At last, I felt his grip begin to loosen.

As suddenly as our war had begun two weeks earlier, it ended. My foe released my hand, brimming with neck, heart, and gizzard. I rinsed him inside and out, massaged him with butter, sage, salt, and pepper, and set him in a pan to roast his rebellious soul.

When my family and I sat to enjoy our meal, at last, the siege was just a passing memory. After all, he turned out to be just a young, tender chicken.

Plastered

In a moment of excitement, Angela volunteered to host and cook a family dinner, a barbecue, on Friday night. As she often did, she'd imagined that something miraculous would happen, that her sisters would finally appreciate and respect her, and that she would gain a new status with her husband. He would, without a doubt, marvel at the fabulous party she'd arranged and be in awe of her competence. That was how she imagined it.

The moment of decision came while at lunch a few weeks before with her four sisters. They'd all agreed it would be fun to have a party celebrating the end of summer, back to school, and the long fall days they loved. They dug in their purses for their calendars and organizers to choose a date. There was no way she would ever remember what she had been thinking though she realized later that she must not have been thinking. Somehow after a few cocktails and very little lunch, she'd been flooded with love for her family and overcome with amazing joy at the idea of having them all together at her house. When she'd volunteered, they'd all smiled and readily agreed. Angela had felt perfect, needed, and capable.

As in all things, the preparation was an enormous job. What gave her the idea that she could do it all with ease, that she had attained the status of an expert hostess? She must have been daft! For starters, she was definitely not excused from childcare because she had things to do. With her kids running round and round in circles, wearing rings in the kitchen linoleum, the planning alone took more than a day.

She found it easier to manage her strategy with a little help from her support group: the multiple bottles of clear, crisp vodka planted discreetly around the house. Here is how Wednesday went:

139

she'd plan, then drink, plan, and drink. Wednesday night, she tried to review her lists with her husband, Stan. At first, he criticized everything she'd planned, but finally, he admitted he wasn't interested and didn't really get the point of all the plans anyway. At that point, she was already bored with them herself. She just wanted another drink.

Thursday morning, after a couple of fortifying shots from the bottle in her shoe box, she drove to the market with her two children strapped in car seats singing at the top of their lungs. She roamed the aisles, forgetting why she was there. When her cell phone rang, she sighed. Undoubtedly, it would be her husband Stan with more instructions. She was right. He reminded her, once again, to buy the things he needed to show off his barbecuing skills. And don't forget the wine! And when she got home, would she rinse off the patio?

Angela traversed the store, her children hanging onto the sides of the cart, weighing it down so that she could barely budge it. Their little fingers clenched the sidebars, and their tiny eyes peeked above grimy knuckles. She paused at the meat case and selected the three biggest hunks of beef available. Then, slowly, she filled her cart with pounds of potatoes, several bottles of wine, ears, and ears of corn, 2 cases of soda pop, a bag of briquettes, two cake mixes, two watermelons, and about sixteen additional items she knew were absolutely necessary for creating a successful event. She unloaded her supplies, mounding them on the moving belt. At the credit card scanner, she paid with plastic. She reloaded the cart with bag upon bag and went out the automatic door. She loaded her kids in their car seats and put her purchases in the trunk. She drove home lightheartedly, but when she got there, she still had to face dragging it all inside.

She found one tip of the bottle was the exact fortification she needed. She put everything away to clear the counters for the work ahead.

After tucking away the receipt to avoid a confrontation later, she cooked: potato salad, deviled eggs, fresh salsa, a couple of cakes, and a wonderful marinade for the roasts. She slid the slabs of beef into huge plastic bags topping each with the marinade and a cup or so of the good red wine she had purchased according to Stan's instructions. She sealed the bags and tested a glass or two of the wine to be sure it was as good as Stan had claimed.

During all the shopping and cooking, her husband called her a total of four times. He wanted to know how much she spent, but she could not tell him because she'd "lost" the receipt. He wanted to be sure she washed the clothes he wanted to wear, that she remembered to rinse down the patio, and once he couldn't even remember why he'd called.

That night Stan threw a stormy little tantrum about not seeing the receipt from Walmart. He said he knew she'd overspent. He counted the bags in the trash. He looked three times in the refrigerator and then at her accusingly. She left the room at last, and he turned silent. Soon the TV was on, and he forgot about money for awhile.

Friday morning, she cleaned. She knew she could not skimp on this. Stan would check everything, and no matter how hard she worked, he probably would find something she'd neglected! She ran the vacuum and mopped the floor. In the broom closet, she came across an unopened bottle of vodka. She broke the seal and took a swig to get through the long day ahead.

As time passed, she dusted perfunctorily, swished out the toilets, and folded the wadded towels. She emptied the dishwasher and wiped down the counters. There was not a quiet moment through all the preparations. Her children were everywhere she wanted to be and into everything she put away. They were so excited to have visitors that they hollered louder, ran faster, and played with more vigor than usual. Everything took longer than she'd imagined. Her memory of past parties was imperfect, she realized. Hosting was a giant pain in the ass.

In the afternoon, she stuffed celery, fixed a plate of olives and pickles, covered it with plastic wrap, and made extra ice. She frosted the cakes and sprinkled on sparkles. She cooled drinks and chopped vegetables for a salad.

Then the sisters started to call her, one by one, to see if she needed help, or so they said. They called, she knew, to check on her, to check her sobriety and her progress. They never had, and would never, trust her to be an adult and plan something independently. The phone never seemed to stay silent long. And she had so much still to do!

In an average week, her most frequently visited bottle of vodka had always been under the kitchen sink. Sometimes just knowing it was there helped domestic activity go more smoothly. On Friday in the late afternoon, she reached down and opened the cupboard before she started her final preparations. In a moment of clarity she thought she might regret her action, but her yearning to soften the edges and give a smooth performance was strong. She was sure one shot would give her that and more.

Vodka eased all turmoil into a mellow haze. Each grating noise became the tinkling of a bell, and her clothes felt like velvet on her skin, and nothing--absolutely nothing--phased her. Instead of having to choose her battles, her mind on vodka forgot there were any battles at all. She tasted triumph with each sip. She felt balanced and extravagantly stylish.

There was a little problem with memory. She mused that her beloved vodka might also have the effect of helping her forget things, things that were necessary or expected. Sometimes things like being ready on time or, now and then, forgetting to have something cooked for dinner when Stan got home from work. Once, she'd forgotten a load of clothes, wet and clumped up in the washer, for four days. She'd often forgotten to return phone calls, make appointments, or bring her grocery list to the store. Nevertheless, things seemed to get done. Somehow. Eventually.

And, yes, there was the question of anger. More anger and hostility popped up lately than at any other time in her life. She was amazed at her instant and violent reactions when something went wrong. But really, the good outweighed the bad. Vodka was her friend, even with these small bumps in the road. And who knew? Maybe it had nothing to do with drinking at all!

So Friday afternoon progressed, and Angela was admittedly feeling less than sober, yet she also felt wondrously expansive and strong. She set up her buffet table with abandon. She used an old lavender sheet to cover the scarred tabletop before she tossed out silverware and plates haphazardly in stacks. A few dozen crumpled and randomly colored napkins landed on the table in a pile. She spent valuable time lost in the garden picking flowers and then in the kitchen arranging them in bottles and Mason jars which she grouped in the center of the table, on the sideboard, and the coffee table in the living room. She stood a moment and admired her work.

The third time Stan called that afternoon, she ignored the phone. Instead, she dragged the kids down the hall and into the tub. She swayed back into the kitchen, bumping walls. Once there, she paused for a quiet moment. Relaxing with her hip against the counter, she had another shot. She sighed and looked around for the list she was sure she'd made. No sign of it. Was there a list? Maybe not. Did it matter? No, really, no. She felt so together; there was no need for a list, really.

Meandering to the end of the hall, she pushed the bathroom door open. She found the twins dripping wet on the bath mat, soap visible in their curly brown hair. She laughed, and they looked up, startled. Catching a glimpse of herself in the mirror, she set to work with lipstick and brush. By the time she left the bathroom, her lips looked wild, but her hair looked tamer. The bathroom she left behind was wet with puddles of bathwater. Hair was in the sink, and the kids had used the last toilet paper. Toys floated in the undrained tub. Towels were strewn wet on the floor.

Her two girls were dressing each other in strange outfits, part pajamas, part church clothes, and as an afterthought, a couple of superhero capes. She didn't care. They were clean, at least. She gave them both big hugs and kisses, startling them again and leaving them with big red lipstick mouths on their cheeks.

She sailed out of their room, stopping at the linen closet. She lifted a bottle from behind the toilet paper packages, took a swig, and continued into her room. She sprayed herself with cologne and found something to wear on the floor of her closet, not appropriate by some standards but very appealing to her. It was glittery, tight, and dramatic. She gathered her hair up with a flowing 8-foot scarf and left the room.

On the way to the kitchen, she glanced blindly at the table she'd set for the buffet. It looked so pretty with all her lovely dishes and the flowers. Entering the kitchen, she looked at the clock, her brain not registering that it was ten minutes to party time. She reached for a glass and dipped under the sink for another quick flush of paradise.

She swallowed and set the glass down. The back door opened, and in walked her cool husband. He was dressed to the nines for his corporate job and showed up just in time to welcome people to a party he'd done nothing to help prepare for. All day he'd made time to phone her a multitude of times. His annoying calls had wasted her time and interrupted her thoughts. If the party was a success, he was sure all his reminders made the difference, that and because he was always the best part of any party.

"Hey, Sugar, is that what you plan to wear tonight?" he asked, looking her up and down.

"Fuck you," she muttered. She had spent a good part of the day thinking glowing thoughts about him and how lucky she was to have him. Now she found it puzzling that he was more like a scoundrel when he came in. Where was the lovely man she daydreamed about? Confused, dumbfounded, very probably a bit drunk, she turned her back and dug around in the refrigerator.

"Did you marinate the meat?" he said. "Did you get the wine I suggested at the store? How about briquettes? Are the kids ready?"

"Yes, I marinated the meat the same way I always do," she said. She slammed a bowl of homemade salsa on the table and reached into the cupboard for some chips. "I got the wine and your beloved briquettes. The kids dressed themselves. And what have you done, Mister? Show up?" She filled a large empty bowl with chips and started eating them. She was famished. Had she eaten today? Had she fed her kids? Her eyes went to the cupboard door beneath the sink. She licked her lips.

Looking up, she was surprised to find him still there! What was he looking at anyway?

"Why do you always try to make me feel bad? Huh? I've been working so hard! Oh, I can't talk to you! Why don't you just go sit somewhere and leave me alone?" She was flushed. She knew she sounded like a big baby. Maybe she sounded like a baby because that's how he treated her! But then, didn't everyone? She shoved her husband, partner, and co-host out of the kitchen's swinging door and walked slowly to the sink. She looked back to see if he was returning. No sign of him. She bent down and poured another drink from the bottle.

The vodka slowly trickled its way down her throat. It felt like burning needles. It felt painfully satisfying. It felt like mounds of spangles were flooding her body. Soon she would rise off the damned kitchen floor and be transported into another realm, a realm of twinkling stars and no responsibilities, a special land where Vodka could be her Daddy, make everything perfect, protect her and love her and praise all her hard work. She could feel that Daddy's infinite smile emerging.

She closed her eyes.

She wanted more.

Two minutes passed before the phone and the doorbell rang at once, and Angela's eyes slowly opened. She steadied herself, hands tight on the edge of the counter.

"Here goes nothing," she murmured. She looked around her kitchen like a stranger and saw a total wreck, a mess that would take more than an hour to straighten. "Oh, no! What will my wonderful, neat sisters think?" she whispered. She could just imagine her kitchen through their eyes. She tipped her glass. Not quite empty. She probed the glass with her tongue. "Fuck," she declared.

Grabbing the bowl of salsa and the chips, she pushed through the swinging door and, trailing her scarf, put on her party face. The flowing scarf caught in the swinging door, but after only a slight yank to her head, she came out without tumbling to the floor and making a scene. Two chips and a little salsa sloshed onto the carpet, but really she was sure no one noticed.

The families arrived, four by six by eight. They brought along their kids, a brother-in-law, two close cousins, and a couple of dogs. They ate chips and salsa and helped themselves to her good wine. She welcomed the noise and confusion, the warmth of bumping bodies. She loved being lost in a crowd, even in her own home. After twenty minutes, no one noticed her. She believed she could just slip in or out, and it wouldn't even matter to anyone. It was such a feeling of freedom!

And so she did just that: She slipped away and planted herself in the kitchen, assuming a dynamic pose. She moved things around and said as little as possible to those who came in to use the bathroom or get a drink. She laughed instead, tossing her head. So much fun, she implied. So great to be ignored, she thought.

After half an hour, her sister Maggie, the oldest of the sisters, came in, talking over her shoulder in her usual bossy way.

"I'll get her off her ass and get this show on the road!" she said. Angela could only imagine which sister she was talking to.

When Maggie turned to the kitchen, she seemed surprised to see Angela standing there. Serenity was her long suit, however. She simply adjusted her face to a smile and asked if she could help. She said,

"It's getting late. We should get something on the table and feed the kids. Can I help you set up?" Angela beamed at her as she envisioned slitting Maggie's wholesome throat.

"Sure," she said. "There's potato salad in the fridge and deviled eggs. Corn on the cob to cook. Watermelon to slice. Salad to toss. There's still a lot to do. Let's just start." In her mind, she

146

dreamed of offering Maggie a drink, having Maggie drink like a fish, and having Maggie make a fool of herself in front of the sisters. She smiled as she turned to the work ahead.

Together they pulled plates and bowls out of the refrigerator and arranged them amid the flowers, napkins, plates and flatware already casually assembled on the table. They put a pot of water on to boil and took out the steaks, lining them up on a platter for Stan to take to the barbecue. Having someone help was motivating, even if it was Maggie. Through the kitchen window, she heard laughter. She wondered briefly what they were laughing about. Probably Stan was telling jokes. He was so good at it! Her family loved Stan.

With a loud bang, the kitchen door slammed back against the fridge. Stan stood there looking beautiful and glowing in freshly pressed shorts and a sky-blue shirt. When had he changed? She smiled. It didn't matter. She was just so blessed to have him! She loved him so much! Even when he annoyed her, she couldn't get enough of him.

Stan did not smile back. She felt her smile tugging at her face.

"I thought you said you got the briquettes!" he barked. She knew everyone in the house instantly stopped talking, moving, and laughing. In the silence only she was aware of, she felt every head turn toward her, her failure exposed. She blushed with embarrassment.

"I got them!" she gasped, sure she had. "I did! I put them in the cart. I was careful." She leaned toward him as if he'd punched her in the stomach. She remembered tossing the bag of briquettes there at the bottom of the cart in the store, she was sure. But then she had no recollection of later lifting them up and into the back of the car. She'd unloaded the kids and stashed bag after bag of groceries in the car's hatch, but the briquettes? She must have just left them in the parking lot, sitting desolately on that wretched shelf under the cart. She'd ruined everything. It was inevitable.

The sun was lowering toward the top of the fence in the back, and with sudden ferocity, a beam slashed through the window above the sink and spotlighted her standing there, staring stupidly at nothing. She felt like a fool. Sudden anger surged through her body. It was Stan's fault. He always asked too much of her! Her face went white, and her hands fell into fists.

"What exactly have you done? What have you done?" she hissed at her husband. "I did everything! What if I did forget the damn briquettes? I did everything else. I did well. Really, really well!" Her eyes fell to the cabinet door under the sink. Her body tilted in that direction. She wanted that vodka so badly. She needed that push to become... to become something bigger, something strong. She needed to regain her importance and her competence. She turned and headed out into the hall toward the linen closet or perhaps the bottle in her shoe box—either would do. As she left the room, she turned and looked at Stan accusingly. "Are you sure you don't have enough briquettes already?" she asked.

Angela went into the bedroom and closed the door. She could hear Maggie talking calmly to Stan. She heard the words "drinking," and "unorganized," and "always." She heard the backdoor open and close, and soon she smelled meat cooking. He didn't even need the briquettes! His purpose had been to persecute her, humiliate her in front of everyone, and make himself a hero.

After Stan headed again to his barbecue, Angela could return to the kitchen strengthened. She continued putting food on the table and setting up glasses and ice in a bucket, sodas, and milk. The meat was done in 10 or 15 minutes. Though she had taken little notice of what was happening around her while working, she saw now that a line had formed at the table. The mood had returned to one of celebration. Her family was jostling for a place, filling plates for themselves and the kids. They were having a good time, giggling and talking.

Stan had sliced the meat and put it on the platter she'd set out for him. He hadn't said a word to her. He would normally have brought in the meat and let her carve it. He must have been avoiding her, which was fine... perfectly fine with her. She wanted to avoid him as well! He made her feel so sad and sorry for everything she'd ever done, for every breath she'd taken as his wife.

She wandered outside, filling her glass with wine from one of the many open bottles on the tables. Her sisters and their families were filling the chairs she'd set up earlier on the patio, the patio she'd spent over an hour hosing down with water. Everything looked pleasant. It looked fine. But it wasn't. It just felt unsettled.

Stan stood at the far end of the patio talking to his brothers-in-law, holding a glass of red wine, wearing his barbecue apron. He was so beautiful. Their two sweet girls played at his feet. She thought back wistfully to how he had treated her when they were dating, when she was valuable to him, even exciting. Something had changed in their life together. She knew that now he felt she would never deserve him, no matter how she tried. She was just unworthy. And she, in turn, avoided him, for heaven's sake! She'd been a poor excuse for a daughter and a sister, and now she'd grown to be less than satisfying as a wife and mother. She could never forget it. He reminded her every day. Her love could not make up for all that she was lacking. All this work, this charade of an event, didn't prove a thing.

She looked up as her fat-butted sister Betty stood up. The bench where she'd been sitting at one of the folding tables visibly rose two inches. She held out her wine glass. "The meat is great, Stan!" she declared with enthusiasm. She looked around, and her sisters agreed, with shaking heads and huzzahs. They all raised their glasses in a toast to the meat and the grill master. Their cheeks were rosy, their bellies being satisfied. They were appreciative. They were, she thought, jerks.

Angela took a step back toward the kitchen door. She watched as Stan lifted his glass in agreement and acceptance. She felt slapped silly, crushed. She'd worked solidly for over two days to put this party together, and all this praise went to Stan for ten minutes of killing red meat on a grill. Her mouth fell open. She went to the kitchen and took a swig from the bottle under the sink. She wanted to slide directly to the floor and die. She felt so betrayed, so sad! Why he had not said, "Oh, no! Angela did everything! You

149

should be thanking her!" She crumpled and wept. She felt invisible, plastered over like a plain blank wall no one even noticed.

Quite suddenly, anger seized her. Why should she take this humiliation? Who were these people anyway? Her sisters? Guests? They had no power here! They had no power anywhere!

She picked up a napkin and blew her nose, then took one step toward the door. She straightened her back and stood tall, her hair hanging loose behind her. She wondered briefly what had become of her scarf. She watched her hand reach out to the handle on the screen door and remembered her hand reaching under the sink for the bottle earlier. She shook her head, and the thought slipped away. She stepped out onto the porch. Put her feet together. Head up. She felt strong as a warrior and had something to say, dammit!

"Excuse me," she said. She was two steps above everyone. She was sure they all saw and heard her, yet nothing happened. Everyone kept laughing, talking, eating, and passing salt and pepper. "Excuse me!" she said again, louder. Still, only a couple of faces glanced her way. Was she transparent?

She bent down and picked up a flat rock from the garden. She smashed it down on the nearest table, a redwood picnic table they'd had since they'd gotten this house three years ago. "Excuse me!" she demanded again.

The violence of the sound caused everyone to look up and some to even put down their forks. She saw Stan look at her warily, then slip from his seat and step toward the bushes at the edge of the lawn. *He's putting distance between us,* she realized. He stayed there and looked at her, shaking his head. She looked back at him as if he were a stranger.

"Ass," she whispered under her breath. She thought she'd whispered, but a little thread of giggling nearby made her wonder.

"Thank you for your attention," she said. She paused, unsure of what to say next. "I would just like to say that I am very happy you're all enjoying your meal," she said finally. "I'm pleased we were all able to get together and celebrate summer and how quickly it's passed and to welcome the Fall that's creeping up on us. But I also want to say that I was pretty shocked when you thanked Stan for standing at the stupid grill for 15 minutes to cook the meat! It's as if he'd added some miracle ingredient to our evening when he added practically nothing.

"Yes, yes, yes, he contributed. Let's see now. He contributed a shopping list of three items, one of which was briquettes that I left on the bottom rack of the cart at the Walmart parking lot, as I am sure you all heard. He also offered advice on my attire. He told you all a few jokes while he was standing around out here before we ate. He made countless phone calls to order me around.

"And finally, here is his big offering: this evening, he stood before the barbecue I cleaned on Tuesday, which had enough briquettes to cook for a small army despite how much he wanted more! He stood there looking handsome with a knife in his hand and a big fork he used to flip the meat onto the grill, the meat that I spent 40 minutes making the marinade and 12 hours marinating. After 8 or 10 minutes, he flipped the steak. Ten minutes later, he hauled the cooked meat off the grill and put it on a plate I'd set out for him. So here's to Stan, the barbecue genius! What a guy!"

Angela lifted her glass toward Stan. Tears ran down her cheeks, and her left hand fisted at her side. She turned back to her family.

"On the other hand, let me just tell you what I've been doing the entire past week to prepare for this event. I am not saying I didn't want the party to happen or wish it hadn't happened here. What I am saying is that I put a great deal of effort into getting this place ready because I wanted it to go well. I wanted you all to have fun and enjoy yourselves. I shopped for the food, cooked it all, cleaned the patio and set up the tables, cleaned the house, picked the flowers, and generally made this party, all with my kids hanging on my legs. And there was the issue of a husband who insulted my every move and demanded that I prepare the meat so he could show off how easily he could toss a steak around in the air and make it land in the same spot, upside down. I know you know this story."

She looked around at everyone gathered there, her house and yard and the lovely garden she planted and cared for. She raised her chin and glared at Stan.

"And so," she continued, "I would like to offer a toast to myself, the one who really put this party together with hard work and lots of valuable time. Here's to me! Here's to me for all I've done to make this a wonderful night. Here's to me for loving every one of you and being so glad you are here to enjoy the evening even though you ran me down and talked behind my back.

"Now, I would like to ask you for recognition. There is no one particular chef in this house. There is not just Stan, who grills meat, but Angela, who cooks everything else while caring for the kids, cleaning, shopping, squirting off the patio and the tables, and making you all feel welcome. Yes, the meat is great. I imagine it is. It always is. But is that a meal? Is that a party, I ask you?"

The patio had gone still. Her sisters knew that what she said was true. She'd heard them complaining about it themselves. The fact was that hostesses were taken for granted. It was a constant source of sadness for wives. They worked hard for every occasion, but then their husbands stood at the grill with a fork, and lo and behold, the flames and the smell of cooking meat were everything! He was congratulated and patted on the back.

On the other hand, they'd always known just what a big brat Angela was. She'd been a foot stomper all her life. She continually proved that she would never cope and never change. Had they expected her to carry this party off? Had they just let her host as a test to see if she could set aside her childish ways and organize something nice? Had they wanted to see if she would pout and throw tantrums as usual, drink all day, and ruin her own party? Angela had had enough.

"Do you all have a drink?" Angela asked from the stairs. "Would you raise your glasses to honor your hostess who put this party together? Yes? No?

"It doesn't really matter. I'll drink for all of you. And speaking of drinks, I'll go to the kitchen now to have one. Or more if I want." She turned and went back into the kitchen.

In awhile, and after much discussion, they forgave her for her behavior as if that were necessary or even in their power. They all understood what she'd said, of course. They'd all lived it! But so what? That's life. And after all was said and done, they knew that as the youngest daughter, she was the most spoiled of the girls, and, on top of that, she often got on these rants when she'd been drinking. And there was a bit too much of that lately, wasn't there? She was just not to be taken seriously, ever, period. They'd known it for years, and she repeatedly proved it.

In the kitchen, crouched on the floor by the sink, Angela overheard everything they said. She'd heard it her entire life, from the top of the stairs at her mother's, the back seat in the car, and the other side of the door when she wept in the bathtub. She was always presumed a failure, and they gave her plenty of chances to prove just that. She slowly rose and walked to her bedroom, the prettiest room in the house, her cocoon, her sweet hideaway. She closed the door and slid to the floor with her friend, her bottle. She raised her glass to the hostess over and over and over again.

Her family stayed and ate and drank and made a mess; they didn't help to clean up. It was quite late when they left. They hugged Stan and told him what a nice party he'd made for them. And oh, please don't feel you have to apologize for Angela! In his exhausted state, Stan threw himself on the couch and fell asleep as soon as he was alone. He snored and dreamt until the sun rose, and the twins fell upon him in glee. He was happy to see them as well. He gathered them up and took them to the car, their outfits still in disarray, and off they went to breakfast.

The house was still a mess, the yard littered with cans and bottles, dirty dishes, and flatware. Napkins were dropped where they were used, and glasses lay tipped on their sides, forming puddles of wine on tabletops. The trashcans overflowed, and the sink was full of serving bowls and pots. Food scraps that even the dog ignored dotted the counters and the floor.

Angela was awake all night in her room, her bottle glinting with each pour. She stared into space like a lost and unhappy little girl and wondered how she could change her life. There were so many entanglements. She was sure to screw that up, too.

"Here's to me," she said, lifting her glass one last time before she passed out on the floor.

A Change in the Weather

Danny couldn't sleep. It was 95 degrees at 10:00 pm. Windows were wide open, and insignificant little electric fans blew hot air into bedrooms all up and down Jasmine Lane. Danny's sheets were damp, his hair wet. A sprinkling of sweat covered the freckles on his nose. The moon was full and hung over the house, lighting it brilliantly and adding swaying shadows to the trains zipping around on the wallpaper in his bedroom.

He could hear his parents in the next room. His mother Pat was talking and talking. Her voice was monotonous. You would think it would lull Danny to sleep, but instead, it irritated him and made him more restless than before his parents had gone to bed. He watched the silhouetted shadow of the elm tree outside dance on his wall as he tried to understand what Pat was going on about. He fiddled with that loose tooth, a molar desperately wanting to be pulled.

Pat was saying something about Danny's sister Sherry. She muttered and blabbed. He could tell she was worried. He strained to hear what she was concerned about. Her voice got louder, and he heard her say Sherry was bored. Sherry's best friend was away at her grandmother's for the entire summer. Sherry needed something to occupy her time, something to focus on. Maybe Sherry needed a sewing machine or a new record player. Maybe Sherry should have her driver's license.

"For Pete's sake! Tell her to get a job so she can keep busy AND buy all that stuff," Danny said out loud. No one heard him, of course. He picked at the scab on his left knee. "It's always Sherry, Sherry, Sherry. If I were old enough to work, believe me, they would

155

have had me out looking for a job yesterday!" Sweat trickled down Danny's neck, and he turned onto his side.

Then the barking started. You could easily hear it over the sound of those insignificant little fans running in every house in town, over the few air conditioners propped in windows, over Pat's ongoing dialog about Sherry. The dog sounded big, and he sounded very unhappy. He howled and then barked. He was quiet for a few minutes, and then he barked again. It was pretty evident that the dog was upset and probably just warming up. He kept up the barking, using howls for punctuation. Danny did not recognize the sound of this particular dog. He didn't seem familiar at all.

A window or two slammed somewhere nearby. Danny's father Earl, got up, his feet hitting the wood floor hard. He stomped across the bedroom. Earl whistled out the window. The dog seemed to recognize the signal. He quieted for a minute or two. Then slowly, he dragged a chain across the concrete. Danny imagined him chained to a post, trying to sleep on cement, his hard hips flat against the hot pavement. A big dog, he envisioned, boney and loose, rising slowly and casting a long shadow as he tipped his head back, ears flopping, as he howled at the moon. Even though his visionary dog was kind of creepy, he felt sorry for him... until the barking began again.

The night seemed to last forever. The heat did not abate, and the dog did not stop his incessant monologue. Hours passed with Danny tossing and turning, watching the moonlight shift from one wall to another. Eventually, the sky lightened, and the sun came up in a burst of orange and pink and other lovely colors which were wasted on the people in Preston. Not one person came out to look at the beautiful sunrise. Everyone was already awake and irritable. The folks on Jasmine Lane were doubly irritated. The barking dog had kept them awake even when they might have dozed off despite the heat.

By the third day of record-breaking temperatures, Danny wanted to jump out the window to a welcome death in the garden below. He was tired and hot, but he was also bored with staying all day indoors, playing with his toy soldiers, building with his Lincoln

156

Logs, coloring in his Daniel Boone coloring book, and running his train set. He wished for a pool or, at the very least, a friend with a friend with a pool. Or maybe he could have a bike that he could ride fast, his T-shirt billowing as he rode to beat the heat. He saw himself cooling off in the breeze he created. He sprawled across his bed, sticky, gross, tired, and bored all at once.

And what about that dog? That great mangy mutt started his barking every night at 9 o'clock. He howled and yapped through the entire night. Tempers were short in the Jenkins household, and Danny knew he had to be quiet and well-behaved, or he would suffer a terrible punishment -- painful and deadly. If asked, he would describe his circumstance easily: Solitary Confinement, just like in prison.

Each day, the Jenkins' big fan droned on in the kitchen. The television, too, was on in the middle of the day, something unheard of in Danny's lifetime. He could hear its staccato chatter from the living room as it hammered down the hall and invaded his space. He was likewise disturbed by the smell of the lacquer in Sherry's nail polish as she applied it over and over to her toes and fingers. His mother wasn't baking -- it was too hot to turn on the oven. She wasn't ironing -- it was too hot to iron. She'd washed clothes on the first day of the heat wave. The first clothes she hung on the line were dry by the time she had finished hanging them all up. He wasn't sure how she was occupying herself these hot days, but he sure missed the aroma of her pies and rich casseroles wafting through his bedroom door.

Danny could hear people heaving things around outside -- trashcans, tricycles, whatever got in the way. With every window open, he was conscious of raised voices in other houses. He heard doors slamming and car engines revving. Kids were whining and crying, and mothers were snapping at them. What he did not hear was anyone calling "Allie, Allie, In Free!" as they ran for the base, playing tag or kick the can. Missing was the shushing of skates along the sidewalk. He heard no music on the air from bird songs or radios or from kids whistling. There were no girls playing hopscotch and none chanting the silly songs they sang when they jumped rope. He didn't hear the bonk sound the basketball made when it hit the

157

backboard above Anderson's garage door, nor did he hear cheering when someone hit a home run out in the street. For those few days, the broadcasting of summer joy was absent from Jasmine Lane.

School was starting soon. His longed-for summer vacation was wasting away in the heat.

On the fourth day, Danny heard some neighborhood men talking outside before they left for work. They were sick and tired of that annoying dog, they said. "Do you know whose it is?" they asked one another. No one seemed to know. Car doors slammed, and the men left, each to his own place of business. It didn't seem fair to blame the unknown dog for everyone's irritation. The heat was the obvious culprit, but that dog, poor soul, was there.

Pat went to the beauty parlor that fourth morning. When she left, she didn't give Sherry or Danny chores to do or any direction whatsoever. Instead, she complained about having to get a perm and sitting under a hair dryer in this heat. "I hope they have air conditioning at the beauty shop," she said. Danny could tell by her face and her voice that she had no hope of any such thing. He kissed her goodbye because he sensed she needed it. "Don't touch me, Danny!" She said. She pulled away and went out the door.

Danny dozed off on the couch sometime after his mother left. Sherry was in taking a cool shower. The running water was a soothing sound. When he woke up, his mother was coming in the door with Chinese take-out boxes in her hands. She was smiling. Danny loved Chinese food, the fragrance of the sweet and sour pork, the crunchy sticks, the little packets of soy sauce, and, best of all, the fortune cookies. He knew his father would complain about the cost, but he also knew that Chinese take-out was the way to his father's heart. Danny sensed some strategy in the works.

"Wow, Mom, why the take-out?" Danny asked her.

"No reason," his mother said. "No reason at all. Would you set the table? Where's your sister?" She set the boxes on the kitchen counter and looked in the mirror by the back door, fluffing her new hairdo with her left hand. The smell of her permanent wave was strong in the kitchen and stung Danny's nose. He grabbed some silverware and escaped into the dining room to set the table.

"I think Sherry's still in the shower. At least she was when I dosed off," Danny called to her. "We tried to work on a puzzle, but sweat dropped on the pieces and it got ruined. Sherry said she'd go and cool off in the shower."

"When your dad gets home, would you send him out back? I have some iced tea for him. Tell him I want to talk to him." Pat seemed distracted. Danny was pretty sure she wasn't listening to what he said. She'd put a little apron on and carried a tin tray painted with yellow flowers. Balanced on the tray were two glasses of tea and a blue bowl of peanuts. The screen door slammed, and Danny could no longer smell his mother's hair.

Earl came in a few minutes later. Danny gave him Pat's message, "I want to talk to him." Repeating his mom's words, Danny had expected his father's reaction to be more worried, but Earl was evidently so exhausted and hot that he didn't need any promises except the cold drink to get him moving. The screen door slammed again. Danny perched on the kitchen stool near the Chinese take-out cartons, eyeing them with desire. He slipped two toy soldiers out of his pocket and set them up to destroy the boxes and free the fragrant food inside.

Outside on the back porch, Pat whispered to Earl, "I met the nicest lady today at the beauty parlor. She and her family are new to the area. They've only been here a few days, maybe a week. She has a son just Sherry's age, and he doesn't know anyone. Well, one thing led to another, and pretty soon Marion, that's her name, suggested our kids should meet. Don't you think that's a good idea? Earl?"

Ice pinged the sides of their iced tea glasses. "That ice must be almost melted by now," Danny said to no one. He strained to hear what his father said. He knew Sherry would have a conniption if she knew what their mother had planned. He could not imagine what his mother had been thinking when she set up this "meeting." His father took awhile to answer. Finally, he must have roused his courage.

"Well, Patty, I'm not sure that's such a good idea. Kids like to make their own friends. Don't you think you should ask Sherry if she wants to meet this boy before you set this up?"

"Oh, Earl, for heaven's sake. Sherry would never say yes. I just have to do it and then tell her. And I have! Marion and I have already set up a date for them. Even if she doesn't like it, I'm sure she'll go anyway and end up having a good time. His mother is so nice; I'm sure he is, too. It's just what the doctor ordered for Sherry's boring summer. She needs something to think about, something to occupy her for awhile. This is just the thing!"

It got quiet out back. Earl set his tea glass down on the picnic table with a thump. He cleared his throat. Danny waited. Nothing happened.

After about 5 minutes, Earl sighed and said, "I see you got a perm today." That set Pat to talking. Danny could imagine his father staring off into space and paying little attention to what she was saying. Danny thought his father was very wise. He felt sure he was learning some lesson from eavesdropping on this conversation, but he had not yet figured out what it was. Something about being a man, he assumed.

Danny slid off the stool. He took placemats and plates to the dining room, filled glasses with milk, and added the bottle of soy sauce to the tray at the center of the table. He stirred Bosco into his milk, sniffed it and took a small sip. He loved the taste of chocolate. He knew his mother would be too involved in the Sherry debacle to notice his unauthorized use of the chocolatey syrup in his milk. He lifted the take-out boxes and set them on the table. Sherry came in the kitchen from the hall in pedal pushers and a halter top. She had her hair piled up in big soft pink foam curlers. Her toenails were the same shocking pink.

"Chinese?" she said. "What's the occasion?" Danny didn't want to get involved. He turned toward the screen door and called to Pat.

"Can we eat now, Mom? Sherry came out of the bathroom!"

160

Danny's parents came in, the screen door slamming behind them. The empty tea glasses slid around on the tray his mother carried. Earl had his suit coat hooked on his finger and flung over his shoulder. His shirt sleeves were rolled up to his elbows, and his collar was open. "I'm with Danny," he said. "Let's eat!"

The Jenkins family sat at the table and bowed their heads while Earl said grace. They passed the little Chinese food boxes around until they had some of each savory dish on their plates. Danny ate as slowly as possible. He didn't want to finish quickly and be excused from the table before his mother unveiled her plan to Sherry. He could feel the tension in the air and didn't think anything this exciting had happened in at least a week. Pat took her sweet time about it. Danny was having trouble keeping any of his dinner on his plate. It was all so good he just wanted to suck it down. About the time he was getting to the point of licking his plate, Pat finally smiled sweetly at Sherry and began her tale.

"I met the nicest lady today at the beauty parlor, Sherry. Marion's her name. She and her family have just moved to town here. She has two or three kids, but the best part is that she has a son just your age!"

Sherry looked up from her plate. She glared at her mother with suspicion. She held her fork full of almond chicken midway to her mouth. The food began to drip from the fork back onto her plate. Still, she did not break her gaze.

"Now, Sherry, honey," Pat said. "You know, I just thought that you might want to meet this young man. He doesn't know anyone in town, and with you being so lonely and bored this summer with Candy being away and all..." She trailed off as Sherry rose from the table, dropping her napkin to the floor and her fork to her plate. Her face was pale, her brown eyes popping. One of the pink curlers had come loose and hung down the back of her neck, clinging to a strand of wet hair.

"Mom! What did you do?" she said. "What did you promise this woman, Mom?" She wasn't precisely shrieking, but that was the word that came to Danny's mind. He thought her body looked like a banana as she leaned over the table toward their mother. Man! She was mad! Little red spots were on her cheeks now. Her hands held the back of her chair so tight that her knuckles were white.

"Sherry, now you know I'm right when I say you've been bored. You know you've been complaining about having nothing to do. Well, Marion and I thought it would be fun for you and her son...oh, what is that boy's name? Derrick? Dwayne? Well, whatever. We thought it would be nice if you showed him a little of what there is to do around here. You know, go to a movie or take a drive and show him the way to school and that sort of thing."

"Mom! I can't believe you would arrange that without asking me! I am not 12. Please. Can you remember I have a brain and feelings? Oh, oh, oh!" Sherry turned abruptly and ran down the hall to her room. She slammed her bedroom door. They heard her hollering in there. She sounded like the midnight dog howling.

"Well," said Pat, "That didn't go too badly, did it?" Danny stared at his mother with her silly tight curls. He wondered what made ladies tick.

"May I be excused?" He asked. No one looked at him, so he just got up and left the table. He took his plate into the kitchen and set it by the sink. It was Sherry's turn to wash. She wasn't getting out of it so easily. He went outside and sat on the front porch. He found some marbles in one of his pockets and scooted his butt down onto the sidewalk, where he knelt and rolled them around, looking at their colors in the sunshine. He was getting a pretty good marble collection.

Sherry wailed and moped for three solid days. Pat did not give in. Sherry was going on a date, and that was final. She took Sherry shopping for a new dress and some dumb summer shoes she called flats. Danny was amazed at how stupid his sister was to waste three days complaining about a date that would last only about 3 hours. He dug a tunnel in the far corner of the backyard and made his soldiers have an intense war in the dirt there. His skinned knee healed. His molar fell out, and no one noticed a thing, even though

162

he whistled a bit when he talked. No money arrived under his pillow. This fairly proved that the tooth fairy was a big fake.

The hot weather continued. It was the longest heatwave anyone could remember. Tempers flared, and raised voices carried more and more frequently from one open window to another as the families on Jasmine Lane felt their nerves stretched to the limit.

And that dog, the Midnight Barker as Danny had come to call him, kept up his long saga of barks, howls, and chain rattling. Sleep remained elusive. No one spotted the dog during the day, but his barking at night made him a local legend, a "spectral illusion," some said. Danny kept his eye out for a chain tied to a post somewhere in the neighborhood. If the weather weren't so hot, he would be out actively looking, but as it was, he searched the best he could whenever his mother sent him to the store two blocks away or when he tagged along with the paper boy just to talk, something to do. No, he didn't find the chain, the cement, the post, or the dog. He daydreamed of being the hero that found the mystery dog, quieted him, and set the neighbors to a good night's sleep. A hero of sorts. That would be him, Danny Jenkins.

But that did not happen. He didn't find the dog, and the barking went on.

After a phone call or two between Pat and Marion, Sherry's date was set. Darryl would pick her up at 6:00 that night for dinner and a drive. Danny wished he were invited. He loved going out at night but seldom got a chance.

The doorbell rang sharply at 6. Danny's mother answered the door. Danny stood in the kitchen doorway, watching to see how Darryl would be. He was good-looking and held his chin up high like he was only looking for things in the air. Danny wasn't sure he would take notice of him if he saw him somewhere, but he bet girls would. He was about 5 foot ten, a little shorter than Earl. He wore a plaid jacket and chinos. He had slicked-back, shiny dark hair and brown eyes, and he wore glasses that made him look a little like Buddy Holly. Danny thought that everything seemed to be okay. Then he zeroed in on the one thing that made Darryl better than just

163

okay. Darryl carried a two-pound box of chocolates. Big! Two pounds! There were flowers for Pat, but he was sure the chocolates were for Sherry.

Danny knew Sherry didn't eat chocolate. She worried about zits, she said. She didn't drink coke and didn't eat anything greasy. "Danny, be careful," she'd say. "You're almost old enough to get zits. Don't eat so much chocolate!" Danny didn't see the point in depriving himself. He ate chocolate whenever it was available. He stared at the box under Darryl's arm. He began to think of Darryl in a new light.

Sherry came down the hall as fast as a snail. She was backlit and looked kind of pretty and grown up. She smelled nice, too. But she wasn't smiling. Darryl turned when she arrived and gave her a slanted smile. Winked. Even with his really nice teeth and dimple, the smile didn't do any good. Sherry was determined to be ...well, Sherry. Darryl handed her the chocolates, and Sherry walked over to the table where the phone sat and dumped the box there. "Thanks," she said.

Danny wanted her to like Darryl. He wanted Darryl to return again and again with more chocolates. So far, it looked like Sherry was not impressed.

Earl came in from the backyard and shook hands with Darryl. He stared down into Darryl's face and said, "Have a good time, kids. Darryl, have Sherry home by 11:30, you hear?" Darryl smiled his dimpled smile, shook his shoulders slightly, and said sure. On the porch, Sherry turned and glanced back. To Danny, she looked like a tiny little girl. She seemed ready to cry. He didn't get it.

"That boy," Earl said as he closed the door, "He's not used to getting turned down. I hope Sherry can handle herself." He went back outside, letting the screen door bang shut behind him. Danny could hear the sound of Darryl's car out front. It was loud, and he took off fast. Danny wasn't sure what his father meant about Darryl, but it didn't sound good. He stared vacantly at the back door for a few minutes and then went off to his room to sweat and look at comic books.

When the sun was low in the sky, Earl came to Danny's bedroom door. "Mom's out playing cards, and there's a World War II movie playing at the theater...Do you want to come out of there and see it with me?" he asked Danny.

"World War II? Why not?" Danny said. So he and Earl headed out to the movie theater, the only one in town that was air-conditioned. If the movie was dumb, there was at least that! The film was black and white, grainy and indistinct. Danny and his father watched together as the GIs got shot and shot back. Guns blazed, men hollered. Danny was amazed at how clean they stayed, regardless of the fact that they were lying in the dirt most of the time. There wasn't much of a story, but there was a lot of action. He felt good that his Dad had taken him along.

After about 15 minutes of shooting, Danny got up to go to the lobby for popcorn. As he opened the exit door, he saw his sister. Darryl stood close to her, looking down into her face. He told her, "Go get us some popcorn and candy." Sherry said something, and Darryl looked angry. He reached into his pocket and shoved money into her hands. Then he turned his back and entered the theater through the door at the other end of the lobby. "Darryl, wait!" Sherry called, but he did not. He left her there and went to watch the show. Danny watched as Sherry tried to compose herself. She finally turned and went to the Ladies' Room. It took him a moment to realize she was crying.

He forgot about getting popcorn and returned to his seat to finish the movie with his father. In the dark, he blushed when he thought about how his sister had been bossed around and abandoned. He didn't want to tell his father. For some reason, he thought that would be like tattling, but he felt he was betraying Sherry by not telling. He barely noticed the movie after that.

At the end of the show, Earl and Danny left the theater, walking slowly up the aisle. Earl was thoughtful. As they walked home together, he looked over at Danny and said,

"Did you notice how the soldiers stood behind one another, Danny? Did you see how when one was hurt, the others carried him back behind the lines? How they would never even stop to consider that move? How they always looked out for each other?"

"I guess so," Danny said. He wasn't sure he had watched the movie closely enough to know what his father was talking about. His thoughts had been on Sherry and her humiliation much of the time the movie played. But he knew his father told him important things, so he tried to understand.

"It's like that in civilian life, too," his father said. "Loyalty is one of man's most remarkable virtues. I hope you will always remember to honor the people who have been good to you, those who inspire or help you, and those who show you they love you through their actions. It's so important to learn how to do that, Danny. Loyalty is a fine thing. A man would not have much dignity without it.

"Know your strengths and use them. Be your own man, son. Be proud of what you accomplish, but don't ever think you've gotten anywhere without the help of others. And don't ever forget them, don't forget those who have stood behind you."

They walked a few more blocks in silence. Danny wondered what in that movie had made his father think these things. Parents got lessons from the weirdest places.

In the quiet, he remembered how his father had looked Darryl in the eye and let him know, just by his look, that if he mistreated Sherry, he would deal with her father. Maybe that was what was on his mind. Whatever it was, he must have wanted Danny to learn something. It would take some thought on Danny's part to figure it all out.

When they got home, his father smiled and said,

"Well, you'd better run off to bed now. Goodnight, Danny." He turned toward his recliner and picked up the newspaper. Danny put his hand on his Dad's shoulder for a second and then went off down the hall to his room. He was pretty surprised that Earl had talked so much. He was generally a very quiet person.

That night the dog didn't bark at 9:00. At 10:00, Pat came home from her bridge game, and by 10:30, all the lights had gone dark on Jasmine Lane except the front porch light at the Jenkins' house.

Danny was rudely awakened at 11:45 pm. The dog had started up again. He was barking fast and furiously. "What got his goat this time?" Danny said, sitting up in bed. Then he heard a voice. It was Sherry's. She was in their parent's bedroom on the other side of the wall. He heard her crying. Not screechy loud like she often did, but softly. Pat was comforting her, but Sherry was inconsolable. Danny turned over and tried to sleep some more. He pulled his cowboy pajama top up over his head to block his ears, but still, he could hear her plaintive voice -- not the words, just the sorrow.

The dog barked. Sherry cried. Pat said so much so softly that she seemed to be humming. The few times he could hear what Sherry was saying, Danny heard his sister say that Darryl wasn't nice and that she didn't want to see him ever again. It upset Danny that this guy had hurt his sister's feelings and hadn't treated her like he should have. She was a nice person!

But it was the middle of the night now. He felt bad that she was sad, but for now, he just wished she would be quiet so he could sleep. Then, at last, Danny couldn't stay awake any longer and off to sleep he went.

For two days Sherry's eyes were swollen. She dragged herself around the house like a broom. Danny heard bits and pieces of her conversations with their mother. Sherry was really insulted by the things Darryl had said to her, as well as the way he'd treated her. Danny never said anything to Sherry about seeing her in the theater. He watched her candidly and tried not to let her know what he knew. He felt so sorry for her. He was surprised to find that he was also embarrassed for her. After listening to all the other mean things Darryl had done, Danny realized that Darryl hadn't just pushed money at Sherry and left her alone in the theater lobby.

167

Darryl had actually been mean and abusive to Sherry the entire evening. Once his mother had heard it all and was convinced Sherry wasn't making anything up, she was as upset as Sherry over how the date had turned out.

And though the phone often rang for his sister, she wouldn't come to the phone no matter what. She was quiet and stayed in her room most of the time. Pat let her call long distance to talk to Candy. Danny was amazed. Long distance was only used for emergencies and very important calls. He had to walk through the room four times to be sure it was Candy she was talking to. On his fourth trip around the telephone table, where the chocolate box still resided, Sherry got fed up with him.

"MOM! Tell Danny to stay out of here while I'm on the phone!" she screamed in exasperation. Lately, everything he did was wrong. Danny wasn't up to being punished for walking around the house! He ran outside to avoid both of them. He threw himself in the grass under the elm tree and watched the clouds in the sky. Wait! These were the first clouds he'd seen in two weeks. They were beautiful. "A sight for sore eyes," Danny whispered. He'd heard that somewhere and it was perfect! Could a change in the weather be coming?

When he thought Sherry would be off the phone, Danny returned to the house on tiptoe. He didn't see her anywhere, but her transistor radio was now playing in the bathroom. He was thinking how he hoped that talking to Candy had helped her when he passed directly by the box on the table.

He opened the lid.

The box was lined with a shiny white paper that was bumpy like a quilt. Inside were two layers of scrumptious chocolates, all smooth edges and nutty lumps, sitting in little individual brown cups. The heavenly aroma of sugar, vanilla, chocolate, nuts, and other yummy goodness suffocated all of Danny's best intentions. He snatched a piece of candy. He smelled it. He put it in his mouth.

168

He heard someone coming! He slammed the lid back on the box and swallowed the candy whole. No one came. He'd wasted the piece of chocolate!

Just one more to make up for the wasted piece, he decided. He chose carefully and bit this one into two pieces. It was all melty, sweet, and rich, and he felt so good. He swallowed the first bite and took the rest in his mouth. He rolled it around on his tongue and smiled. Chewed. Swallowed that piece as well.

"Sherry is never going to eat this stuff," he said to himself. "She doesn't like chocolate, and she doesn't even like Darryl. I could eat a few more, and she would never even know!" He opened the box, took out two more pieces, slid them in his pocket, and went to his room. He opened his desk drawer and put them inside, covering them loosely with paper. He looked out the door. No one was coming. Sherry's radio still played in the bathroom. He went quietly towards the front door, but passing the box again was very hard. He stopped and looked at the white paper cover with the drawn-on bow. He sniffed the box. "One more piece to take outside," he said. He seized another piece and went out the door.

Danny spent the day under the elm tree thinking one minute about Sherry and her sorrow and then, the next minute, that "just one more piece" would not matter. Ultimately, he'd taken about 18 pieces of chocolate, each considered "just one more." His stomach hurt. He headed inside to lie down in his room. As he passed the box, he looked inside and discovered he'd eaten about half of the top layer. He realized that to hide what he'd done, he would have to buy another whole box. Or he could just hide this one and hope no one ever wanted it for anything. Since he had no money, Danny chose to hide the chocolate box.

He walked around the house looking for his mother and his sister. His mom was out in the front yard yacking with Mrs. Cook from across the street. They were looking up at the clouds with smiles on their faces. Mrs. Cook said something, and they both started to laugh.

Sherry was nowhere to be seen. She was lately like a ghost, not there and then suddenly there but, at the same time, kind of see-through and vague.

Danny took the box off the telephone table and slid it under his T-shirt. It did not fit. He looked around again and went out the back door but did not let it slam. Scanning the yard for somewhere to hide the box, he spotted the tunnels he'd dug for his soldiers at the end of the garden. "I'll bury it!" He said.

It was easy to turn the tunnels into a nice-sized hole. He set the box down in the bottom of the hole, careful not to dump out the precious contents. For a minute his stomach, full of chocolate, rolled and tumbled. He thought he'd be sick, but it passed, and he was okay. Even so, his stomach continued to groan and rumble. He was sitting back on his heels with both hands full of dirt, ready to cover up the box when his mother called him from the back porch.

"Daniel!" She hollered. Danny jumped sky-high. "What are you doing out there in the dirt? You're wearing your new T-shirt! Get in here right now and change. I need you to take out the trash and set the table for dinner." Danny looked down and realized that, unlike the soldiers in the movie whose clothes never got dirty even when they hung around in the dirt, he was a filthy mess, and it had only taken a few minutes!

He quickly threw dirt over the top of the candy box. As he left, he looked back just once. To his dismay, he could see a shiny white corner of the box wasn't covered. Though he planned to return after dinner and do a better job, Danny was too sick to go outside after dinner. He spent the evening lying on his bed, moaning.

At nine o'clock Danny was in his pajamas, in bed, waiting to fall asleep. That's when he realized the heat wave had broken. The house was miraculously cool. And music! He heard music! A neighbor was playing the piano! He heard Mr. and Mrs. Cook out taking a walk, talking and laughing as they made their way up Jasmine Lane. Moods were lifting. Danny felt a weight lift from his heart. It had been a long time since he'd felt his sheets cool against his legs. It seemed forever since his hair hadn't been stuck to his

170

forehead. And even though his stomach wasn't well and his sister was miserable, Danny felt pretty good.

The big dog started barking right about then. He barked furiously for about 10 minutes. Then the barking stopped. In the silence, Danny heard the dog's chain snap, and its full length hit the concrete at once. Then nothing. Danny hoped that the dog had run away. He wanted to get a good night's sleep for once. He thought about Sherry for a minute and remembered how she used to sit with him when he had a broken leg and then about a time she'd chased away some mean kids who were bullying him out in front of the house. He thought about what his Dad had said about loyalty. He guessed that was the kind of thing he meant--someone helping you or doing something nice for you when you needed it. Sherry had her good points, he decided.

Danny dozed. Danny snored. Danny dreamt long and involved dreams full of chocolate, dogs, soldiers, and immense digs. The night passed, cool and quiet, while Danny's stomach gradually settled. Jasmine Lane returned to its previous state of well-being. Or so it seemed.

At seven o'clock in the morning, Danny heard someone hollering. A lady screamed. He tried to go back to sleep, but the commotion did not abate. He finally got up, tore off his pajamas, and pulled on shorts and a shirt. He ran outside to see what was going on.

The ruckus came from his backyard. Down at the far end of the garden, Darryl and the screaming woman were standing over an enormous grey dog on his back, his legs stiff up in the air. At first, the dog didn't look real. As Danny got closer, he saw it was a big dead dog. He was the ugliest dog Danny had ever seen.

"Darryl?" Danny said as he came up to the two people. "Is this your dog?"

"Danny?" Darryl said, looking up. "Danny, this is my Mom, and this is her dog, Missy. Poor Missy. Something killed her in the night!" He put his arm around his mom, Marion, and held her while she cried.

"Wait just a minute," he said. He was looking around the end of the garden, pushing dirt with his shoe. "There's part of a box here. Let's see what it is." He bent to pick up the remains of the candy box Danny had buried the day before. Danny was struck dumb. He didn't know what to say or what to do. He looked at Missy and saw that her entire mug was covered in chocolate, her tongue was hanging out the side of her mouth, and the teeth he could see were brown and muddy looking. "Chocolate killed Missy," he thought. "I killed Missy!"

For once, Missy was quiet. Her barking was stilled for eternity. Danny was sad that Missy had died from the chocolate. Even though he didn't care for the barking, Danny loved most dogs. He did feel some guilt for stealing the chocolates, but he found he just wasn't sad that Missy was now done barking. That part of Missy he could live without.

Darryl looked up at Danny from where he crouched near the hole Danny had hurriedly dug the day before. He looked puzzled. "This looks like the candy I gave Sherry the other night. What's it doing out here in the yard?"

Darryl had made his sister cry for three days straight. Danny did not care to explain to Darryl that he himself had left the candy out where it could kill Darryl's mother's dog. Of course, he'd not killed her intentionally, but essentially what he did was kill Missy. "Well, I'll be darned," was all Danny could say.

Then he turned and ran for the house.

"Come here, you brat!" Darryl called after him. "Come back here and tell me what happened to this candy! Did you take this box of candy from Sherry? This candy cost me plenty. You brat!" Darryl's mother wailed on about her dog, and Danny ran inside and slammed the door. Sherry stood in the kitchen doorway, her eyes wide, and her mouth open. The room seemed quieter than a tomb. "Danny? What's the matter?" she said, her eyes as big as saucers.

172

Danny thought for a moment. He remembered what his father had said about how a man has to have dignity, and he has to have loyalty. He thought about how Darryl had treated his sister so badly that she had cried for days. He thought about how downright mean Darryl was. He thought about how the weather had changed and realized he had changed himself. He said to his sister,

"Nothing is the matter, Sherry. Not one thing." Then he went back outside to face Darryl. He knew he would be loyal to his sister until death. He knew it was a fact and he didn't need to prove it, but he would, nonetheless.

At the bottom of the garden, Darryl and his mother stood over the stiff dog, the Midnight Barker, who had gone silent. The mother was still hysterical. But Darryl's fists were squeezed up tight as they hung by his sides. His face was red, and all his features were pushed together in the center, wrinkled up, and mean.

Danny turned to Darryl's mother. "Ma'am," he said, "I'm sorry about your dog. And I'm also sorry that you have Darryl for a son." He then turned to Darryl.

"Darryl," he said, his hands on his hips, feet set firmly on the ground. "This poor lonely dog was annoying. She barked all night, every night. You could have come out to see what was wrong or to calm her. You never cared about her or how she kept everyone on the block awake night after night. And yet you are suddenly so upset. That just doesn't make sense." Standing uphill on an incline, he could look right over Darryl's head. After a moment of silence, he pulled his shoulders back and his chin up.

"You came into town thinking you were something special, but then you made the mistake of taking my sister out and treating her worse than you treated this dog here. And now you have the nerve to stand around and holler at me.

"Darryl, take your ugly dead dog and get off our property. Go home and don't come around here again. You and your expensive chocolates, you and your neglected dog. The Jenkins can live very happily without you."

173

Danny remembered how his father had looked down at Darryl when they met, how he had spoken to him and looked him in the eye. Danny looked Darryl right in the eye. Then he turned his back on Darryl and his mother and their lump of a dog and went back up the hill to his house. He walked tall. He felt tall.

"Well," he said to Sherry in the kitchen, "I am happy to say that the Midnight Barker won't keep us all awake with his nonsense anymore. And don't you worry about Darryl, Sherry. He won't be calling you up or coming around here making you cry anymore. You're too good for the likes of him to begin with." Danny looked at Sherry when he spoke. He was glad he was on the same side as his sister.

"Really?" Sherry said, her cheeks turning pink, her eyes shining with tears about to fall. "Oh, I hope you're right, Danny!" Danny nodded. He could say no more without crying himself. Sherry came over to him. She hugged him. He was embarrassed but also amazed because Sherry's hug--the one he'd so often avoided--felt so exactly right.

It's Mom Again

I close the book on my finger to keep my place and haul my ass off the couch to answer the damn phone. Caller ID: It's Mom. Again.

"What is it, Mom?" I'm brusque, I know, but she has called incessantly since Dad died last year. Sometimes it doesn't seem she needs anything but attention. Often I am patient, but then other times, I'm not.

"I've fallen," she says. I strain to hear her. Holding a breath, I picture her apartment.

"Where are you?" I say. "How bad is it?"

"I'm stuck between the counter and the island in the kitchen." She gasps. "It's bad this time, Bev. I know it."

"Okay. I'm coming. I'll call you an ambulance. I can't lift you myself."

"Okay. Just hurry!" She actually whimpers. "Please," she whispers.

"I'll be right over! Be as still as you can." I press END to hang up the phone. I stick a scrap of paper in my book, dropping it on the table. I turn to the minuscule expanse of my mobile home.

"Holy shit!" I holler. "What can happen next?"

When Dad took to falling, I learned never to go to bed without half a tank of gas in the car and never to put on pajamas until I was crawling into bed. My two rules have saved me time and again. I was out of there in 5 minutes.

175

The senior park where I live has speed limit signs posted on every street that say "10 MPH" in large black print. I break the limit on every block, bouncing over the ridiculous speed bumps in my rush. I've arranged the ambulance, and now I am calling the apartment manager from my cell phone in the car.

When I arrive, I hear Mom howling as they gently lift her onto a stretcher. The pain must be real or she would save the crying for me. It breaks my heart. The pulsing light from the ambulance flashes through the blinds like a lighthouse on speed. The manager, in robe and slippers, greets me with big frightened eyes.

"It's okay, Sharla," I say. "This was bound to happen, I guess. She's so unsteady on her feet these days. You can go back home, but thanks for letting the paramedics in."

"She's grown so small," Sharla says. "I almost didn't see her on the kitchen floor when I let myself in. I've never known Evelyn to make a scene, but she's not holding back tonight, is she?" I nod, and she leaves. I forget about her.

Another neighbor appears at the open doorway. "What's going on?" she demands. I shut the door in her face.

It's cold in the apartment. It's obvious she wasn't able to turn up the heat. I imagine Mom down on the floor before it got dark, alone, unable to reach the phone. She'd have had to crawl to get to it.

They wrap three blankets around her. She's in shock and shivering, pale as the moon. The paramedics are gorgeous knights in shining armor. Must be a slow night—they sent us six strapping young men. They are solicitous and sincere.

We confer. I look for Mom's medications and bundle them into a plastic bag to take along, then lock up and follow the ambulance to the hospital.

By the time I park, the paramedics and hospital personnel have whisked Mom into the Emergency Room. I go to the waiting room, which is so aptly named. Tonight it's filled with the waiting sick and their families and loved ones. Everyone is restless -- rustling, wiggling, moaning, stretching, and sighing in the plastic chairs. I am told to join them. They say they will call me when I can go in. I don't believe it.

I sink into a chair and regret that in my rush I left my book at home. I borrow paper, draw pictures, write words, and finally, a poem. Time moves so slowly that I step out of it and float.

I hate this big ugly room full of glare and plastic. People are sneezing, coughing, and barfing. Babies whine and cry, and kids scuffle and fling a blanket or a toy on the floor. Grown people pretend to read, search purses and backpacks, use their cell phones, and whisper. Old crumpled magazines are tossed on the chairs. A stack of newspapers on the floor looks like badly folded laundry. One man opens his laptop purposefully, stares into space, then closes the lid—not one key touched. The harsh lights flicker. We are, as a group, lost between day and night. There's no telling what time it is. We're rattling around together in a box named WAIT. A bunch of strangers; we don't even have a common cause.

"Beverly Simon," a nurse calls at the door. I hesitate – maybe I don't want to know. But my legs respond, and I find myself standing in front of her. I think briefly of gin. She leads me through a wide door and down the hall to an empty room made of fabric and a bed. She brings me a chair and leaves me.

I've been waiting in Mom's little drape-defined cubicle for 30 minutes when they roll her back in from X-ray. She looks strange—pale-faced, her hair all fluffed out and wild, not her usual pin-curl-look. I am puzzled by her disappearing lips. She seems colorless.

The ER is noisy. One man continues to yell about his pain. Nurses converse and laugh absurdly off in some distant place. Gurneys, lab carts, and machines pass by. Through a space between the curtains, I see them rushing along.

Everyone looks determined to appear busy. The phone rings and rings. A cold draft drifts around my feet. Doctors glance at clipboards, huddle outside the curtains, and then vanish. I can see their feet, can hear their shuffles.

The beeping of Mom's monitor begins to slow. Her sheet moves very little when she breathes. I get worried and step out to ask for help. Suddenly all the people are gone, working diligently on some urgent project. I am told, "I'll send your nurse right in." An hour later, I am told, "We're waiting for results." Two hours later, a doctor steps between the curtains that make up the room's walls. He talks but doesn't seem to say anything. His job is to check Mom in or to send her home, not really to dispense medicine.

When he leaves, I turn to Mom,

"I think I need some coffee. How about you? Would you like me to bring you anything, Mom?"

"No, dear, I'm too tired to think. Just go and let me sleep." Her mouth barely opens to let the words leak out. The light shines down on her face like a beacon. I look at her monitor with its tiny mountains and valleys. When I glance at her again before I pick up my purse, she has slipped off to sleep. I've loved her all my life. I kiss her forehead.

I stay away as long as I can. Maybe 20 minutes? Returning, I find a commotion around Mom's bed. I hear TV words like "Clear" and "Flatline." What the hell? I leave her for a few minutes, and… Pandemonium.

When next I can see through the white coats and scrubs to Mom's bed, she is lifeless with a sheet pulled up to her chin. Everyone has stepped away and returned to work with their heads down except one busy nurse disconnecting the machines crammed into the little space. No one has spoken to me! I stand by the bed and try not to get in the way. I touch Mom. She's cold.

"We did everything we could," the nurse finally says, not meeting my eyes. "She was left on the floor for too long. She had internal bleeding from many broken ribs. She just couldn't make it."

I am now the one in shock. I can't think of one thing to say. I shiver. My mind is working, but it's not making sense. I want to yell at this woman. I want to bellow, "What the hell do you mean? Where is my mom?" I don't get it. I just don't.

And here is Mom, like a piece of furniture. They can just wheel her away. If I wait long enough, they will. They'll be calling her The Body.

I stand by her, holding her cold hand in mine. The nurse continues to fold up cords and wipe off surfaces.

"Wow, Mom," I say. "I just went for coffee." Then I begin to cry.

NED 2095

My identification number is 2XLG49P0G. I am twelve years old. I live on the 22nd floor in building GN47 in City No. 762. Oh, yes, I have a name as well—it's Ned.

In my computer mail the other day, I received a message from my paternal grandparents. They told me that my Father was assigned to write his life story when he was my age. It was called an autobiography. Back then, boys had to go to a building away from their homes called a school. They went each day for education. My Father had to take this assignment to his school and give it to his instructor. After the instructor assigned it a grade, it was returned to my father. He took it home to a house which he shared with his parents. They were so pleased with it that they put it away so I could read it someday. Of course, they did not know if I would ever exist, but they were hopeful that I would and that I would enjoy reading this autobiography. I don't know a great deal about my father.

My grandparents have offered to mail me my Father's assignment so that I may read about my parent's childhood. Since my grandparents were very poor, they could not afford to provide a computer for my Father's studies, and he could only use a very old typewriting machine to prepare it. I have to wait for the city mail to bring it. That could take a long time since the mail is seldom used anymore. Even if he had used a very old-fashioned computer, I could have downloaded it in just minutes. This seems very unfortunate to me! I am very anxious to read it.

While I await this document, I thought I would use my recreational time to write about MY life for MY child to read one day. When I discussed this idea with Jacob, he agreed it would be a good thing for me to do. Instead of telling the story of my life, however, I have chosen to tell about my daily life in my twelfth year, which is pretty much my life's story since it changes only a little

181

each day. This is the most exciting year I have had so far. I hope that someday a child of mine will enjoy reading it.

A TYPICAL DAY IN MY LIFE

By Ned, 2XLG49P0G

My AI companion, Jacob, wakes me up each morning by singing in my cubicle. This is not a human voice but the sound of water falling, wind blowing, and synthesized violins. It is very soothing and does not cause me to jar awake. After I tell Jacob what I want to eat for breakfast, I go into my bathing area and am showered and blown dry. Then I go to cabinet 3 in my cubicle, and inside I find the clothes Gaultier has chosen for me to wear for the day. Usually, I wear some soft pants and a matching shirt. The material can keep me warm, but that is usually unnecessary since Jacob keeps my cubicle at 74 degrees which is very comfortable.

The robot assigned to my corridor, Gaultier, brings me my breakfast, and I usually eat it in front of my monitor. I am very fortunate to have a large monitor. It is almost like having a window in my cubicle. Sometimes I set it for Outdoor Viewing and watch as vehicles pass or snow falls. I can also watch the news while I eat or call up a friend on the Internet and pretend to eat together. I don't do that often because I am used to eating alone.

After I've eaten my breakfast and have put my dishes in cabinet 5, I meditate. I can do this as long as I want, but I usually lose interest pretty fast. I mainly choose to meditate because I know that it helps me stay in control of my emotions and my body. I can play music using Jacob's many talents while I do this. Some days I choose to do stretches instead. These are equally recommended.

When I sit down for my studies, I am always glad if I do the stretches. I have to sit with Jacob for about 4 hours without a break. He teaches me almost anything I want to learn. I have certain things required of me, but I can sometimes get him off on a tangent and learn about what interests me.

This year I have been asking him about Geography. It is an old science about the Earth and the people who live on it. I can never remember being out of building GN47, so I have many questions about the Earth and the people. Jacob seems to know everything. He is never impatient with any of my queries. He can connect to computers worldwide, and I can talk directly to them. They tell me about the local customs, food, dress, language, and government. It is a very good way to learn, and Jacob is never jealous if I want to ask the foreign computer many questions. In fact, he always remembers the answers in case I forget! Gaultier was a big help to me when I was studying France. He is programmed to understand only French and knows all about France as if he were from there.

Sometimes I try to stump Jacob with my questions. I don't know why I bother since he always knows the answers, but sometimes his answers make me laugh. For instance, he had a very hard time describing the feeling of rain to me. I was laughing uncontrollably as he explained. But in the end, I did not know if he had told me the truth or made it up. I do not know if Jacob likes me. I do not know if he can.

After completing these 4 hours of intense study, I talk with Jacob about what I would like to eat for lunch. Then I jump up and down about two dozen times to relieve tension. When I was younger, I had a trampoline for this purpose, but now my cubicle is smaller, and I only have a mat. I check my online mail for messages. Sometimes I get messages about club meetings to be held later in the day or personal messages from others in the building. When Gaultier brings in my lunch, I plan my afternoon while I eat. Then Jacob enters my schedule into the building calendar so my whereabouts will never be questioned.

After lunch, I am entertained and educated simultaneously with classical music, plays, and operas on my monitor. Sometimes Jacob reads to me from the classics. I can also read these books on the monitor, but I usually close my eyes and let him read to me because my eyes are so sore from the morning's studies. Now and then, he takes me on a tour of an important museum. Once, we did the Louvre in Paris, France, and another time he showed me the Smithsonian in Washington, D.C. I get a great view of the display, art, and statues because my monitor shows no people, and the museums are silent except for Jacob's voice. Sometimes he shows me old parks, mountains, and sea videos. I also like the animal shows he puts on my monitor. I find animals very curious.

With lunch, rest, and relaxation over, I have to study some more. I usually try to do the easy things in the afternoon because I am slower then. I am not sure I should call this "afternoon" since GN47 has very few windows, so we are never really sure what time of day it is or even what season it is. We depend on our computers to keep us up to date. Once or twice I have thought about how computers could rule our lives by making us think that night is day and day is night and mix us up so badly that we would be their pawns. Trust is something I think about now and then. If Jacob wanted to confuse me, this would be the time of day to start.

I am very quiet and lazy after lunch and entertainment. So we do philosophy, trigonometry, or computer science, which are all pretty easy for me. I think I was born with a computer chip in my brain. The study and use of computers are such elementary subjects for me that it seems I have been at this forever! This study period is shorter--only about 3 hours long. Then I am free!

I go down to floor 18 for my exercise. By this time I really need it!! I run laps for about 45 minutes, or I swim for awhile. I am not much of an athlete, but after sitting so much of the day with Jacob, I am anxious to get moving. We have basketball courts and tennis courts on floor 6, but I barely ever go there unless I am going to watch a game. I enjoy watching a hockey game on floor 32 more. Sometimes I plan that for my after-dinner outing. All of the event schedules are easily available through Jacob. I check them carefully when I plan my afternoons and evenings.

At about 5:00 pm, I eat my dinner in my cubicle. This is usually my favorite meal of the day since it is always a hot meal and comes to me with dessert! The food I eat is very good for me. Jacob always tells me the good things about what I ask for before he tells Gaultier to bring it to me. He wants me to be sure I have chosen what I think I need and want before it is prepared. In GN47, we do not like waste. Also, I am required to make sure that I have a well-

184

balanced meal plan. Jacob has been very helpful to me in learning how to do this. If I forget something, he will be sure I ask for it by the end of the week.

We have an Inter-action Center on the 15th floor. I try to go there for at least half an hour daily to appear social. I am not very well versed in the ways of others and so am not very comfortable in human contact, but I try. Jacob says that I must learn about people, and this is the way to do it. Most of my friends are friends on the Internet only. We write each other messages--jokes, riddles, plans, sometimes games or studies—or we contact and chat with each other on the monitors. That is as close as most of us are used to getting. The ones who do the contact sports live elsewhere. They go to a common center for education. They learn together because they do not study well alone with their computers. My friends and I are being trained for special things. Our destinies are not yet known to us.

At the Inter-action Center, I sometimes watch a movie with others. It seems funny to hear laughter during a silly scene. Usually, my laughter is the only sound I hear when something funny happens in my cubicle. We can also watch tapes of old-time car races at the center. They are pretty funny, but we are shocked at how fast the cars move. The vehicles we see on our monitors when we look at what's happening outside are square and slow. Hardly anyone goes out or moves about in a vehicle except delivery people. We seldom see anyone move very fast except at sports events. Our lives are quite sedentary. All of that activity is very emotionally taxing for us.

No one talks very much to one another at the Inter-action Center. On the GN47 internet, there is a board where you can post messages, and many of us use it to communicate with someone we have met at the center or even online. Most of the people who live and work in Building GN47 are fairly quiet. We spend so much time alone that silence never bothers us.

I have to sleep at about nine or 9:30 since I am due to get up and study each morning again. When I return to my cubicle, I undress and drop my clothes in cabinet 5, from which they are collected for the building laundry. Then I go to bed. Before I ask Jacob to turn out the lights, I always look at the pictures of my Father

185

and my Mother on the monitor. Jacob dims the monitor but keeps these pictures on all night in case I wake up. I don't remember ever doing that.

And that is the story of my days. They are all pretty much the same. We don't have holidays which I understand were very important in old times. I have some contact with the outside world, but generally, my life is contained in my cubicle, with Jacob and my studies. Now and then, I wonder about my Mother and Father. My grandparents know who I am, but I don't know them. My Father and Mother died in a rebellion ten years ago or more. I don't remember them at all. I have lived here as long as I can remember. Life is very curious.

Call Center Changes

Imara was down on her knees, leaning forward on her forearms and searching under the desk for the back of her earring. It was dark under there. She continued to talk to Mr. Jones, her customer, about his bad credit as she ran her long fingers through the brown shag carpet. Her big purple-skirted butt was sticking out from the leg hole of her workstation.

Sam the Snake oozed on up the aisle. He spotted the back end of Imara inching out of her cubicle. He assumed she would never know who was there, so he helped himself to a little pinch. The little pinch didn't seem like enough of a percentage feel for a large backside. He tried a sly pat. By then, Imara had screamed so loud that the unsuspecting client, Mr. Jones, had probably gone deaf in his left ear.

As she tried to back out of the little space under the desk, she hit her head on the bottom of the drawer, and her headset tumbled off into the dark recesses, pulling her hair down around her eyes. Once free, she rose to her full 5 foot 11 inches. She hauled off and clobbered Sam the Snake, a good one. His bag of Doritos went flying in all directions. For good measure, she belted him again. Why didn't he go down? Imara packs a punch.

Sam was aghast! He had no idea how or why this woman became offended. She, after all, had presented herself to the main aisle of Cardiff Credit Call Center. She didn't let him wonder long, however.

"You nasty little excuse for a man!" she hollered into his upturned face. "Whatever made you think you can just come here and take liberties with my DARE-E-AIR?"

By this time, heads appeared over the little carpeted room dividers that separated the desks into cubicles. Some observers were still on calls, chatting animatedly with customers while they watched. Others were standing with their mouths open, eyebrows raised. And then there were those eating chips and cookies with no life in their eyes. Eventually, they glanced around at one another and shrugged.

Sam tried his damnedest to avoid Imara's fist. She continued to flail about, her voice rising dramatically as her temper soared. More heads popped over the top of the dividers. No one seemed to be working.

Maureen, in the cubicle next to Imara's, called the supervisor from her house line. She told him to get the hell out of the break room. That something big was going down. Bert agreed only when he heard Imara over the phone line hollering at Sam,

"You are one stupid man. Don't you know better than to touch a female at work? I can sue you for that, you dummy."

Two women employees, Sandra and Joanna, started to applaud. Jamal whistled, and Juan raised his right fist and yelled, "You go, girl!"

Bert finally appeared at the end of the aisle. The quiet office he'd slipped out of a few minutes before had become a thing of the past. Paper balls were flying; everyone was standing, waving their arms, and cheering or jeering. It was pandemonium. He wondered if anyone was taking calls. The call queue on the wall showed at least two dozen calls waiting. His workforce was out of control.

When Bert left the office, Marianne and James had gone out on the porch to smoke. Finished, they opened the back door, letting in a smoke cloud. They were amazed that no one seemed to have noticed they were gone. Quietly they tiptoed back in and took a good look at the situation: the office in disarray, employees cheering, calls waiting, chips on the floor, and Imara hollering. Sam the Snake looked small and alone.

Meanwhile, Bert approached the warring workers. He thought he would try to talk sense into them. Sam hid behind Bert while Imara continued to yell and taunt him, hair flying and arms raised to emphasize her anger. She stamped her foot which caused the floor to tremble. Bert backed off.

Imara was now in control. There was no doubt. Everyone waited to see what she would do next. Though she was a strong girl, she'd never been in this position.

She was so pissed off that she had tears streaming down her cheeks, a real girl thing. Looking around, she suddenly became aware of her surroundings. She had an audience of idiots who lined the tops of the dividers like pumpkins on a fence, staring and wondering what she would do next. She knew she had to make a decision.

Why hadn't her boss done anything? It was beyond her. Dumb old Bert—how did he ever get to BE her boss anyway? All he wanted to do was hide out in the break room. He had never confronted any situation. He never told anyone that what they were doing was wrong. He was like a piece of linoleum, square and dull, just there to walk on.

She could have just walked out. She could have. But she wouldn't. She needed her job! She could have slugged that damned Snake again. But that wouldn't accomplish anything. She turned to Bert and said,

"Bert, get in your office. I have something to say." Bert obeyed her without a word. He just followed her. She pushed the door shut and turned to him.

"Bert, you are the worst goddamn manager I have ever worked for. That man out there is a scum and should have been fired years ago. I can't believe you have stood up for him all this time. He's a tiny little person with no morals and no work ethic. That makes you even smaller. How does that feel, you ridiculous excuse?

"We have a situation here. I don't like it, but you walked out and let it happen. This is what we're gonna do. I hate this call center. I hate the smell of my cube mate's body odor and potato chips. I hate the gossip and the politics. I prefer not to mention the customers. I hate the dark and boring little rooms we're stuck in day after day, prisoners of collections, and the length of our headset cords. But I need to work. I know I can do your job better than you can, so this is what we are going to do. You are going to let me do your job. If you don't, I'll sue this company, and you'll lose your crappy job. So get out of my way. I'm going to be your assistant today and your boss next week."

She bent over Bert in his squeaky chair, and he crumbled.

"Whatever you want, Imara. I'll do whatever you want. Here, take these keys. Do you want a desk? Do you want your own phone line?"

Bert looked around for more things to offer Imara. He was willing to give her anything she wanted. If truth be told, Bert did not love his job then or ever. He was happy to hand it over. Tomorrow he might change his mind, but today she could have his job and his life. He didn't want to get in trouble with the big guys. But even more, he just didn't want Imara to give him a knock on the head.

"Get out, Bert," Imara said. "Go make your employees do their jobs. I'm taking over this desk and this job. Do you hear me? GET OUT THERE!" Bert backed out of the office and turned to face his crew.

"Get to work, you sons of bitches," Bert yelled. Heads ducked slowly behind the carpeted dividers. Whispering stopped. Eyes faced directly ahead. No one believed this was over, but somehow, somewhere, some imagined how life might change tomorrow.

190

About the Author

When Judy Gorham sits down to write she is often inspired by the many different people she has met over the years. Her focus is on short fiction and poetry which she has been writing all her life. She divides her time between Vancouver, Washington and the Long Beach Peninsula on Washington's coast. She lives with her husband, artist Gregory Gorham, and her associate, assistant and accomplice the beloved Cavalier King Charles Spaniel, Ozzie. Visit her website judygorham.com to know more about Judy!!

Made in the USA
Monee, IL
13 November 2023

46454755R00114